ALSO BY

MAURIZIO DE GIOVANNI

*The Crocodile*

*Blood Curse:*
*The Springtime of Commissario Ricciardi*

*Everyone in Their Place:*
*The Summer of Commissario Ricciardi*

*The Day of the Dead:*
*The Autumn of Commissario Ricciardi*

*By My Hand:*
*The Christmas of Commissario Ricciardi*

*Viper:*
*No Resurrection for Commissario Ricciardi*

*The Bottom of Your Heart:*
*Inferno for Commissario Ricciardi*

*The Bastards of Pizzofalcone*

*Darkness*
*for the Bastards of Pizzofalcone*

# I WILL HAVE VENGEANCE

Maurizio de Giovanni

# I WILL HAVE VENGEANCE

## THE WINTER OF COMMISSARIO RICCIARDI

*Translated from the Italian by Anne Milano Appel*

Europa Editions
214 West 29th Street
New York, N.Y. 10001
www.europaeditions.com
info@europaeditions.com

This book is a work of fiction. Any references to historical events, real people, or real locales are used fictitiously.


Fourth printing, 2016

Original title: *Il senso del dolore. L'inverno del commissario Ricciardi*
Translated from the Italian by Anne Milano Appel under the license of Hersilia Press. 

Library of Congress Cataloging in Publication Data is available
ISBN 978-1-60945-094-6

de Giovanni, Maurizio
I Will Have Vengeance

Book design by Emanuele Ragnisco
www.mekkanografici.com
Cover photo: Vittorio Emanuele Prince of Naples
(Naples, February 12 1937) © GBB Archive Contrasto
Digital elaboration: Papirus

Prepress by Grafica Punto Print—Rome

Printed in the USA

To my mother

# I

The dead child was standing motionless at the intersection between Santa Teresa and the museum. He was watching two boys who were sitting on the ground, playing *Giro d'Italia* with marbles. As he watched them, he kept saying, "Can I go down? Can I go down?"

The man without a hat knew the dead child was there even before he saw him; he knew that the boy's left side was intact while on the right the skull had been crushed by the impact, that the shoulder had been driven into the thoracic cavity, staving it in, and that the pelvis was twisted around the broken spinal column. He also knew that a small balcony was closed off on the third floor of the corner building that cast a chill shadow on the street that early Wednesday morning, a black cloth still draped over the low railing. He could only imagine the sorrow of a young mother who, unlike him, would never see her son again. She's better off, he thought. All this anguish.

The dead child, half obscured by the shadow, looked up when the man without a hat passed by. "Can I go down? Can I go down and play?" he asked him. A three-storey fall, a blinding pain quick as a flash. He lowered his eyes and hastened his pace. He passed the two boys who went on playing their game, their expressions serious. Poor children, he thought.

Luigi Alfredo Ricciardi, the man without a hat, was Commissario of Police with the Mobile Unit of the Regia Questura di Napoli. He was thirty-one years old, the same number of years that marked that century, nine of them under the fascist regime.

The child, who had been playing alone in a courtyard of the family home in Fortino, in the province of Salerno, one July morning a quarter of a century ago, was not poor. Little Luigi Alfredo was the only son of Baron Ricciardi di Malomonte; he would never have any memory of his father, who had died quite young. His mother continually suffered from nerves and died in a nursing home when he was a teenager, studying at a Jesuit college. His last image of her was her dark complexion, her hair already white at just thirty-eight, and her eyes feverish. A tiny woman lost in an oversized bed.

But it was that July morning that changed his life forever. He had found a piece of wood, which his fantasy transformed into the sabre of Sandokan, the Tiger of Malaysia. Mario, the steward of the estate with whom he spent long hours, wide-eyed and breathless, was an enthusiastic fan of Salgari and his stories were quick to become reality. Thus armed, the boy had no fear of ferocious beasts or enemies, but he needed a jungle. There was a small vineyard adjacent to the courtyard, where he was allowed to go. He liked the shade of the broad vine leaves, the unexpected coolness, the hum of insects. Little Sandokan, bold with his sabre, advanced into the darkness, prowling silently through his imaginary jungle. Instead of cicadas and hornets he pictured colourful parrots, and he could almost hear their exotic calls. A lizard dashed across the path streaking the gravel; he followed it, bent slightly forwards, the tip of his tongue protruding, his green eyes intensely focused. The lizard veered, changing its course.

Sitting under a vine, on the ground, he saw a man. He was in the shadows, as if seeking respite from the fierce heat of that stifling July in the jungle. His head inclined, arms hanging loosely at his sides, hands resting on the dusty earth. He seemed to be asleep, but his back was rigid and his legs, stretched out on the path, were somewhat disjointed. He was dressed like a farmworker, but as if it were winter: a wool vest, flannel shirt with no collar, heavy pants tied at the waist with a cord. Little Sandokan, sabre in hand, registered those details without noticing anything out of place. Then he saw the handle of the large pruning knife sticking out of the man's chest, on the left side, like the branch of a tree. A dark liquid stained the shirt, dripping to the ground, where a small puddle had formed. The Tiger of Malaysia saw it clearly now despite the shade of the vines. A little further on, the lizard froze and was eyeing him, almost disappointed at having the chase interrupted.

The man, who must have been dead, slowly raised his head and turned to Luigi Alfredo, with a faint creaking of vertebrae; he looked at him with filmy, half-closed eyes.

The cicadas stopped chirping. Time stood still.

"By God, I didn't touch your wife."

It wasn't because of the unexpected encounter, or the handle of the pruning knife or all that blood; Luigi Alfredo ran away screaming because he wanted to leave behind all the sorrow that the farm laborer's corpse had showered on him. No one ever told him that the crime that had occurred in the vineyard five months earlier was the result of another worker's jealousy. The man fled after killing his young wife as well; they said he joined a group of bandits in Lucania. They attributed the child's fright and terror to his excessive imagination, his solitary temperament, and the gossip of the local women who sat sewing under the window of his room in the evening, seeking a breath of cool air in the courtyard. They referred to it as the Incident.

Luigi Alfredo became accustomed to using that same word when thinking of what had happened to him: the Incident. Since the Incident had occurred . . . As the Incident had made him realize . . . The Incident that had oriented his existence.

Not even his *tata* Rosa, the nanny who had devoted her entire life to him and who still looked after him, had believed him at the time. Her eyes grew sad and then a flicker of fear appeared, as though she had a premonition that the little boy too was destined to suffer the same malady as his mother. And so he understood that he would never be able to speak about it to anyone, that he was the only one who bore this mark on his soul: a sentence, a damnation.

In the years that followed, he set about defining the limits of the Incident. He saw the dead. Not all of them, and not for long: only those who had died violently, and only for a period of time that revealed extreme emotion, the sudden energy of their final thoughts. He saw them as though in a photograph that captured the moment their lives ended, one whose contours slowly faded until they disappeared. Better yet, he saw them as in a film, like those he sometimes saw at the movies, only the same scene kept playing over and over again. The image of the dead man, bearing the marks of his wounds and his expression at the very last moment before the end; and his final words, repeated endlessly, as if to conclude something the soul had begun before being torn away.

He felt their emotion more than anything else. Each time he grasped their sorrow, their surprise, their rage, their misery. Even their love. On nights when the rain beat against his window and he couldn't get to sleep, he often recalled a crime scene where the image of a baby, sitting in the washbasin in which he had drowned, reached out his little hand toward the exact spot where his mother had stood, seeking help from his own murderess. He had felt the baby's unconditional, absolute love. Another time he was confronted with the vision of a man's corpse, stabbed by an insanely jealous lover at the moment of orgasm. He had seen the intensity of the pleasure and had had to leave the room hurriedly, pressing a handkerchief over his mouth.

This was what the Incident, his life sentence, was like. It came upon him like the ghost of a galloping horse, leaving him no time to avoid it; no warning preceded it, no physical sensation followed it except for the recollection of it. Yet another scar on his soul.

# II

Luigi Alfredo Ricciardi was of medium height, and slim. He had a dark complexion, striking green eyes, black hair slicked back with brilliantine: sometimes a strand or two came free, falling over his forehead, and he distractedly smoothed it back in place with an abrupt gesture. His nose was straight and thin, like his lips. His small, almost feminine hands were restless, always moving. He kept them in his pocket, aware that they betrayed his emotion, his tension.

He didn't need to work, thanks to a family income that he didn't care all that much about. And as some relative would remind him during rare summer visits to his hometown, he should frequent a society more suited to the name he bore. But he kept both the income and the title to himself, so he could remain as unnoticed as possible and go about the life he had chosen—or, rather, that had chosen him. You try it, he would have said if he could; you try to feel all that sorrow, relentless and unremitting in all its forms. Constantly, each and every day, seeking peace, demanding justice. He had decided to study law, completed a thesis on criminal law, then joined the police; it was the only way to acknowledge those demands, to lighten that burden. In the world of the living, in order to bury the dead.

He had no friends, he didn't associate with anyone, he didn't go out at night, he didn't have a woman. His family ended with his old *tata* Rosa, now seventy years old, who served him with absolute devotion and loved him dearly, though she never tried to understand what it was he saw or what he was thinking.

He worked late, isolated from his colleagues who took care to avoid him. His superiors feared his qualities, his extraordinary aptitude to solve seemingly impossible cases, his total dedication to his work: features that made one think of unbridled ambition, a determination to stand out, to climb the ladder, to step into someone's shoes. His subordinates didn't understand his moroseness, his silences: never a smile, never a superfluous comment. His methods were unconventional. He did not follow procedures, but in the end he was always right. Those who were more superstitious—and in that city there were many like that—sensed something unnatural in Ricciardi's solutions, as if his investigations proceeded backwards, as if he went over the course of events in reverse. It was natural that the officers assigned to work directly with the Commissario would react with a scowl of irritation. Moreover, his investigations did not rest: once begun, they ended only when the case was solved. Night and day, even Sundays, until the offender was in jail. As if, each time, the victim were a relative of his; as if he had known him personally.

Some appreciated the fact that he systematically refused the special monetary incentives awarded for the more important investigations, turning them down in order to benefit the squad. Also that he was always present, even giving up his days off. And he kept his subordinates' mistakes from the eyes of their superiors, covering up for them himself, though he later confronted the responsible party bluntly, reminding him to pay more attention. Still, only one of his co-workers was genuinely attached to him: Brigadier Raffaele Maione.

Having recently turned fifty, Maione was very glad to be still alive and in good shape. In the evening, at the table, he was fond of repeating to his wife and five children: "Thank the Almighty God that you have food to eat. And thank your lucky stars that your father hasn't been killed yet." And his eyes would quickly fill with tears at the thought of Luca, his oldest son who had entered the police force like him, but who had not been so lucky. In service for a year, he had been stabbed to death during a search in the Rione Sanità district, in Naples' old historic centre. The pain was still fresh, even though three years had passed. His wife no longer spoke about him, as if that strong, handsome son—who was always laughing and who would take her in his arms and make her go flying and who called her "my girl"—had never existed. And yet there he was, planted squarely in the centre of her heart and soul, displacing his brothers and sisters, and accompanying her throughout the day.

Maione had become attached to Ricciardi at the time of his son's death. The then deputy of police had been among the first to arrive on the scene. Gently, he had asked Maione to leave the tavern where the boy's body had been found, lying in a pool of blood, the knife protruding from his back. Ricciardi had then remained in there alone for a few minutes, and when he came out of the darkness his green eyes seemed to gleam with an internal light, like those of a cat, but they were full of tears. He went over to Maione. In the silence of those present, men embarrassed by the father's anguish, Ricciardi reached out and squeezed Maione's arm. Maione still remembered the unexpected strength he had felt, the warmth of that hand through the fabric of his uniform.

'He loved you, Maione. He loved you very much. He called out to you, it was his final thought. He will always be with you, with you and with his mother.'

Even through the haze of his immense sorrow, Maione felt a chill down his spine and at the back of his neck. He had not asked, either then or later on, during years of surveillance operations or the long trips required by various investigations, how Ricciardi knew, why he had been the one to deliver his beloved son's final message. But he felt that that was exactly what had happened, that the deputy had told him what he had seen and heard, that they were not the usual words of comfort that he himself had so often repeated to families of the deceased.

That's when Maione had become attached to Ricciardi. In the terrible days that followed, without respite or clemency, nights and mornings and afternoons and evenings without eating, without drinking, without going home, he chipped away at the neighbourhood's unbreachable wall of *omertà*, its code of silence, trading information, even promising to look the other way when it came to certain trafficking, just to get their hands on the vile murderer from the tavern. In the end, even Maione, though fuelled by rage, had to give in to exhaustion. But not Ricciardi, who was gripped by a fiery passion, as though possessed.

And they had caught the killer: in another neighbourhood, still in possession of the stolen goods, surrounded by his accomplices. He had laughed when they burst in. The lookouts he had stationed at the end of the alley were already bound and under guard. A twelve-man operation: there wasn't one policeman who didn't want to get his hands on Luca Maione's killer. When the storeroom had been emptied of accomplices and stolen loot, the man, finding himself alone with Ricciardi and Maione, begged them to spare his life, whimpering and no longer the cocky thug he had been. Ricciardi watched Maione. Maione stared at the man and saw his son as a little boy, bringing him a ball made of old rags, laughing, his face dirty and his eyes shining. He turned and left the room without a word. It was then that Ricciardi had in turn become attached to Maione.

From that moment on, Maione was Ricciardi's constant companion. Each time the Commissario went out, it was he who briefed the squad that was to escort him. He knew that during the first inspection of the crime scene Ricciardi had to be left alone. It was up to him to keep out the other cops, the witnesses, the sobbing family members and curious onlookers, during those first long moments when the Commissario was getting to know the victim, focusing his legendary intuition, and tracking down the fundamentals needed to begin the pursuit. Then too, he acted as counterpoint to Ricciardi's silences and solitary nature, thanks to his innate affability and his ability to communicate openly with people. He was solicitous of the perils the Commissario went up against, always vulnerable, with a boldness that sometimes seemed reckless or even suicidal. Maione suspected that Ricciardi went in search of death, of its quintessential meaning, with an inquiring frenzy, as if to define it, to reveal it; with no particular interest in his own survival.

But Maione didn't want Ricciardi to die. First of all because, in his good-natured simplicity, he was convinced that a part of his lost son lived on in the Commissario. Then too, because over time he had become fond of those silences, those brief smiles, the echo of sorrow that could be seen in the gestures of those tormented hands. And so he continued to watch over the Commissario's well-being, on Luca's behalf and in his memory.

## III

In the chill wind of that Wednesday morning, Ricciardi was walking down from Piazza Dante, hands in the pockets of his dark grey overcoat, head hunched between his shoulders, eyes on the ground. Moving briskly, he could hear the city without looking at it.

He knew that on the way from Piazza Dante to Piazza del Plebiscito he would cross an invisible boundary between two distinct realities: below, the wealthy city of aristocrats and the bourgeoisie, of culture and entitlement; above, the working-class neighbourhoods in which a different system of laws and regulations applied, equally rigid or perhaps more so. The sated city and the hungry one; the city of feasting and that of despair. How many times Ricciardi had witnessed the clash between those two sides of the same coin.

The boundary was Via Toledo. Old buildings, silently facing the street but noisy in the back: windows thrown open on narrow alleys, the housewives' first songs. Church doors, their façades wedged between other buildings, opened to welcome the faithful who went to commend the day to God. The wheels of the first buses rumbled over the large stones that paved the street.

Morning was one of the very few times when mingling occurred: from the warren of alleys in the Quartieri Spagnoli, street vendors came down along Via Toledo with their carts of assorted goods and hearty calls; from the densely populated port districts and from the outskirts, skilled craftsmen, shoemakers, glovers and tailors went up towards the maze to reach the burgeoning residential district of the Vomero or the shops lining the dim alleys. Ricciardi liked to think that that was a moment of reconciliation, of interaction, before the awareness of disparity and hunger led some to be consumed with envy and contemplate crime, and others to fear an assault and crack the whip.

At the corner of Largo della Carità, as on the last several mornings there, Ricciardi saw the image of a man who had been the victim of a pickpocket: he had fought back and had been savagely beaten with a stick. Brain matter oozed from the crushed skull and blood covered one eye; the other still flashed with rage, and the mouth with its broken teeth kept repeating incessantly that he would never let go of his things. Ricciardi thought about the thief, by now impossible to find, swallowed up by the Quartieri; about hunger, and the price paid by the victim and his killer.

As usual, he was the first to arrive at the Questura. The policeman at the entrance snapped to attention in a military salute and Ricciardi responded with a brief nod. He didn't like walking through the crowded halls of the municipal headquarters once life at Palazzo San Giacomo reached the mayhem and bedlam stage, or making his way through the detainees' venomous invectives, the guards' loud calls to order, the lawyers' strident arguments. He much preferred the early morning hours, with the still-clean staircase, the silence, the nineteenth-century feel.

When he opened the door to his office, he noticed the familiar smell as he did every day: old books, prints, a bit of dust left by time and memories. The leather of the old desk chair, of the two chairs facing the desk and of the worn olive-green desk blotter. The ink in the crystal inkwell set in the letter-holder. The pale wood of the desk and the overflowing bookcases. The lead grenade fragment brought back to

Fortino by the old war veteran Mario, once used in so many imaginary battles as a child, now a dubious paperweight. The sun's light forced its way through the dusty windowpanes, reaching the wall and illuminating the portraits like a divine investiture.

"Such beauties," Ricciardi quipped to himself with a half-smile. The little king without power and the great commander with no weaknesses. The two men who had decided to expunge crime by decree. He still remembered the words of the Questore, a dapper diplomat whose life was dedicated to providing absolute satisfaction to those in power: "There are no suicides, no homicides, no robberies or assaults, unless it is inevitable or essential. Not a word to the people, especially not to the press: a fascist city is clean and wholesome, there are no eyesores. The regime's image is granitic, the citizen must have nothing to fear; we are the guardians of assurance."

But Ricciardi had understood, long before studying it in books, that crime is the dark side of emotion. The same energy that drives humanity can divert it until it becomes infected and festers, then explodes in brutality and violence. The Incident had taught him that hunger and love are the source of all atrocities, whatever forms they may take: pride, power, envy, jealousy. In all cases, hunger and love. They were present in every crime, once it was pared down to its essentials, once the tinsel trappings of its outward appearance were stripped away. Hunger or love, or both, and the pain they generate. All that suffering, which he alone was a constant witness to. And so you, my dear *Mascellone*, Ricciardi thought sadly, gazing at *Il Duce*'s protruding jaw, can issue all the decrees you want; unfortunately, however, you and your black suit and debonair hat will not be able to change men's hearts. You might manage to frighten the populace rather than make people smile, but you won't change the dark side of those who continue to experience hunger and love.

Maione appeared in the doorway, after a discreet tap on the door frame.

"Good morning, sir. I saw your door was open. Here already? Can't sleep well, even with this cold weather? Spring doesn't seem to want to come this year. I told my wife, we can't afford the cost of wood for the stove for yet another month. If this weather keeps up, the kids will get chilblains. And how are you this morning? Shall I bring you a so-called coffee?"

"Same as usual. And no thanks, to the coffee. I have a mountain of reports to complete. Go on, go. I'll send for you if I need you."

Outside, amid the first cries of the street vendors, a tram rumbled by and a flock of pigeons flew up into a still-wintry sun. It was eight o'clock.

# IV

Twelve hours later, the only thing that had changed in Ricciardi's office was the light: the dusty desk lamp with its green shade had replaced the anaemic late-winter sun. The Commissario was still bent over his desk, busy filling out forms.

More and more often he thought of himself as a clerk in the land office, obliged to spend most of his time transcribing words and listing numbers: the accounting of the offence, the rhetoric of the crime.

He had succumbed to hunger around two, going out in the cold without an overcoat to get a *pizza fritta* at the cart downstairs from the station; the dense smoke from the pot of boiling oil, the inviting smell of fried dough, the warmth of the glowing hot crust, had always been irresistible to him. This was one of those moments when he felt the city nourished him like a mother. Then a quick espresso in Piazza del Plebiscito, at Caffè Gambrinus, as usual, watching the passing trams with their typical cargo of jubilant street urchins in tow, balancing on the rails, clinging to the coach.

As his frozen fingers clutched the hot cup, a little girl came up to the window, pouting. Hanging limply at her side in her right hand was a bundle of rags, perhaps a doll. Her left arm was missing: a fragment of white bone protruded from the torn flesh, splintered like a piece of fresh wood. Her hip was staved in, her chest cavity crushed. A tram, Ricciardi thought. The girl stared at him then, all of a sudden, held out the rag doll to him:

"This is my daughter. I feed her and bathe her." Ricciardi set down the cup, paid and went out. Now he would feel cold for the rest of the day.

At half past eight, Maione appeared at the door again.

"Do you need anything, sir? I'd like to go, my brother-in-law and his wife are coming to dinner tonight. I ask you: don't these two have a house of their own? They're always on my back."

"No, Maione, thank you. I'm leaving too in a little while. I'll finish up here and close up shop. Goodnight. See you tomorrow."

Maione shut the door again, but not before letting in an icy draft that made Ricciardi shiver, as though it were a premonition. And it must indeed have been a premonition, because not even five minutes had gone by when the door opened again to reveal Maione's burly, thickset figure.

"Forget what I just said, sir; just when I wanted to leave on time for once. Alinei called from the front door, on the intercom. There's a young man. We have to go see, he says something terrible has happened at the San Carlo."

# V

Don Pierino Fava had arrived at the usual side door at seven in the evening, as agreed. It was the entrance to the Palazzo Reale gardens, the Royal Palace, where Lucio Patrisso was the caretaker. An important friendship. Not that he was more lenient with Patrisso than with his other parishioners, nor did he give him any special considerations. Still, it was an honour for the man to receive a personal greeting when leaving church after Mass.

This reasonable price bought don Pierino the greatest pleasure of his life: the opera. His simple heart would soar and accompany the voices, as his lips silently followed the librettos he knew by heart. From the time he was a child, in Santa Maria Capua Vetere, not far from Caserta, he would sit on the ground in the garden of a villa where a phonograph bestowed magic in the air. He could sit there for hours, heedless of cold, heat or rain, listening with bated breath, his eyes brimming with tears.

Small and plump, with dark, lively eyes and a prompt, contagious smile, he had intelligence and a quick wit that greatly worried his parents, farmworkers with eight other children. What would they do with this clever, lazy boy who always came up with excellent excuses to avoid working? The answer came from the gruff parish priest, who called on him more and more often for small tasks just to have the cheerful sprite around. And so little Pietro became "Pierino from the church." He liked the cool shadows, the heady scent of the incense, the sun's rays filtering through the tall stained-glass windows.

But most of all he liked the cavernous, rumbling sound of the great organ, which he had come to consider the voice of God. And when he realized that he would never want to live anywhere else, he felt called. During the years of study that followed, Pierino's love for his fellow man, for God and for music remained intact, and he divided his time among these three passions, assisting the poor, drawing examples and lessons from the lives of the saints, and cultivating sacred music.

By the age of forty he had been the Assistant Pastor of San Ferdinando for ten years, a parish that was not large, but densely populated. It included elegant streets and the majestic Galleria, but also the hovels of the Quartieri and the maze of alleys above Via Toledo. In the centre of the district stood another temple, which exerted a pagan attraction on don Pierino's simple soul: the Royal Theater of San Carlo. He would never admit it, but the theater was the very reason why he had always humbly told the diocesan Curia that he did not feel capable of becoming a pastor somewhere else. He considered it a personal gift from God that he was able to witness the magnificence of the opera's living art, feel its crystalline ringing, and see human passions performed with so much beauty and power. How present God was in the tears and laughter that he saw on the faces of the audience in the orchestra, in the tiers of boxes, in the gallery; and how much human love and divine grace there was in music that led souls by the hand to places the mind could not reach.

So don Pierino was quite content to continue being the Assistant Pastor to old don Tommaso, who imposed no limits on his immense energy. Much loved by the street urchins, whom he let tease him about his squat appearance, he was nicknamed *'o Munaciello*, the little monk, after the legendary mischievous sprite. But he was also known for his frequent denunciations of epidemics fostered by shameful sanitary conditions in the Quartieri. He could be forgiven this one weakness and granted three hours of joy a couple of times a month. The good Lucio Patrisso was there to see to this. For don Pierino's purposes he was the most important man in the parish's jurisdiction. The priest saw to it that the eldest son of the theater's caretaker studied a bit of mathematics and the man let him in through the entrance to the gardens on opening night. His spot was a narrow space behind the curtains from which he could watch the performance unseen. A unique perspective, which the priest would not have traded for anything in the world. And in fact he was there even on 25 March 1931, when Arnaldo Vezzi was killed.

Ricciardi did not like the opera. He didn't like crowded places, the tangle of souls, sensations, emotions. The way they influenced one another, turning the crowd into something completely different from the individuals it was composed of. He knew from experience what an animal the crowd could become.

Then too, he didn't like the theatrical representation of emotions. He knew them well, better than anyone else, he knew how they lived on in those who experienced them, rising in a wave that overwhelmed everything in its way. He was well aware that emotions never came in just one flavour, that a passion was never limited to the most obvious aspect; that for better or for worse there were a thousand facets to it, always unexpected and unpredictable. As a result, he was contemptuous of those colourful costumes, those modulated voices, those archaic, cultured words in the mouths of poor devils who were actually starving to death. No, he did not like the opera. And he had never been to the Royal Theater. Still, he knew how it looked from the outside: on important evenings the festive atmosphere of expectation was palpable even to those just walking by.

As he left the Galleria, heading a small team that included

Maione and three policemen, Ricciardi found himself at the top of a short flight of marble stairs leading to the street. There he saw the usual panorama: the imposing Royal Palace, the elegant portico through which one entered the theater, and to the right, the lights of Piazza Trieste e Trento, its cafés teeming with life and pleasure; the suffused sound of music and laughter. To the left, past the Angevin Castle and the trees of Piazza del Municipio, the rumble of the sea at the port.

The area in front of the theater, however, was not how it usually was. And the difference was jarring.

Hundreds of people were crowded around outside the main entrance, standing in an unnatural silence. Heedless of the biting wind that whistled through the narrow portico, elegantly dressed men and women in long silk gowns huddled in their overcoats, their gloved hands holding on to their hats to prevent them from flying away. Children in tatters stood on tiptoe, their bare feet suffering from chilblains, to catch a glimpse of something. Not a whisper, not a word. Only the wailing of the wind. Even the horses, harnessed to the carriages that waited in the street, refrained from snorting or stamping. And there were no cries from the street vendors with their carts of roasted chestnuts and sweets. The gas lamps that adorned the theater's façade shed dappled light on the crowd, revealing fur collars, fluttering scarves and wide-eyed stares eager for details.

The arrival of the men from the Questura had the effect of a stone thrown into a placid pool of water. The crowd parted to make way for them and a chorus of voices rang out asking what had happened, what the trouble was, why the police were late in arriving, as usual. A couple of kids attempted a timid applause. In the spacious theater lobby, its lavish opulence illuminated and warmed by brightly lit chandeliers, Ricciardi was surrounded by journalists, theater employees and spectators, all talking at once and therefore incomprehensible. Then again, he and Maione both knew from long experience that any really useful information would have to be pulled out with some effort, battling all kinds of reservations. So it was useless, if not detrimental, to listen to that cacophony of words shouted in the excitement of the moment.

Ricciardi identified among the others a little man in evening attire who was bouncing up and down like a coiled spring, sweating profusely. The uniformed staff were looking at him worriedly and the Commissario imagined that he might be the theater manager.

"Deputy . . . or rather, Commissario . . . such a tragedy . . . " the man stammered incoherently. "Such a thing . . . here, at the San Carlo . . . I must tell you, that never, never! As far back as anyone can remember . . . "

"Calm down, please. We're here, now. Tell me, you are . . . ?"

"Why . . . I'm Duke Francesco Maria Spinelli, the director of the Royal Theater of San Carlo. Didn't you recognize me?"

"Truthfully, no. Please, lead the way. Let's get out of this confusion," Ricciardi replied coldly. Meanwhile, the three policemen and Maione had their work cut out for them trying to hold back the swarm of curious onlookers who crowded around. The director took the response as a slap in the face and his expression changed from agitated to offended. Two waiters in livery looked at each other, stifling a laugh, and were frozen by a dirty look. The little man turned with haughty grace and headed for the marble staircase packed with people who stepped aside as he passed, like the Red Sea parting before a dwarfish Moses.

# VI

Patrisso, the caretaker at the entrance to the gardens, looked around cautiously.

"Quick, don Pieri', come in. Don't let them see you, because if they catch me here letting you in, right on opening night, I'll be in all kinds of trouble. Run, hurry up, you know where you have to go."

Don Pierino smiled, happy as a child in a pastry shop. With unexpected agility, hiking his gown up over his ankles, he hastily climbed the main staircase, turned right first, then quickly left into the corridor of the tier of boxes, and took the narrow stairs leading to the stage. There he stopped on a small landing and squeezed into a niche from which he could see, on one side, the corridor with the dressing rooms and the stairs used by the actors, and on the other, most of the stage. He had to crane his neck and stand on tiptoe, but the view was unique and extraordinary: alongside the singers, facing the audience, but also, if he wished, facing the never-ending work that went on behind the scenes. Holding his breath, he was preparing himself. This was 'his' evening.

Not because of the programme, to tell the truth. *Cavalleria Rusticana* and *Pagliacci* had a certain charm, but the most important thing was that tonight he would again hear the celestial voice of Arnaldo Vezzi, the world's greatest tenor. Vezzi was undoubtedly the star of the season's playbill. His role, Canio in *Pagliacci*, was not the best. Don Pierino would have preferred him in a Puccini performance, which would have allowed the subtle nuances of his rich, full tones to find the right resonance. Still, the Assistant Pastor suspected, no other role had the exposure that Canio had with respect to the other parts. The score of Leoncavallo's opera allowed Vezzi to perform practically on his own, to command the stage without anyone overshadowing him.

The orchestra had entered, accompanied by loud applause. The audience of San Carlo loved its "masters," who were among the best in the country. Directing the musicians was Mariano Pelosi, an elderly conductor of great interpretative rigour. Three taps of the baton on the lectern, his two hands raised: the magic had begun.

At the top of the marble staircase with the red velvet runner, Ricciardi, not pausing, whispered to Maione to send the policemen to close off the entrances, the main one as well as the secondary ones. None of those present were to leave the theater. The little theater director led them through a back corridor and up some narrow stairs to a landing with a small door on the left and two doors straight ahead. Along a corridor on the right, other open doors could be seen.

"This," said the Duke, indicating the little door, "is the stage manager's office. The one opposite is the orchestra conductor's dressing room. And there . . . such a tragedy . . . in my . . . in *our* great theater . . . "

Ricciardi looked around to register as many details as possible. The last door the theater director had indicated had been taken off its hinges. There were fragments of wood on the floor and the lock, still secure, dangled, almost completely torn off. The doorjamb showed visible damage: the door had been forced from the outside, you could tell by the position of the doorknob and by the distorted bolt. All around them, a colourful crowd: the Commissario saw clowns, common folk in Sicilian regional costumes, Calabrian peasants, Harlequin and Columbine. He felt the onset of a severe headache. On top of it all, the place was overheated and he was wearing a heavy overcoat.

"Who broke down the door?" he asked.

"I did," said a large, heavyset man with red hair and a dishevelled look. "I'm the stage manager, Giuseppe Lasio."

"Who alerted you?"

"We did. We came to bring him his costume. We knocked for five minutes, we called out, but no one answered." The person who had chimed in was an imposing, middle-aged woman, wearing a blue smock and a pair of large scissors hanging from a ribbon around her neck. At her side was a young woman struggling to hold up a dress-hanger which held a large, very colourful clown's costume.

"Don't let anyone move until I come out of the room. Maione, see to it."

Maione knew what he had to do: he went to the unhinged door, looked inside the room, made sure there was no one in there and said, "Stand back, all of you. Commissario, it's all yours."

Ricciardi went to the door, lowered his eyes and stepped inside.

Don Pierino, halfway through *Cavalleria Rusticana*, was pleasantly surprised. The opera was actually a side dish, or rather an appetizer, for *Pagliacci* and the appearance of the great Vezzi. The Assistant Pastor, like many others, was so eager to see the tenor's spectacular display that he would have gladly reversed the canonical order of the works. Instead, to his amazement, the singers of *Cavalleria* were giving a brilliant performance. The tenor who played Turiddu, the soprano in the role of Santuzza and especially the baritone, Alfio, seemed in top form and eager to make a good impression in the presence of such a talent. Even the orchestra was proving to be equal to the task, and their execution, having now arrived at the chorus following the musical intermezzo, was evolving from noteworthy to memorable. Don Pierino was so moved by the poignant music that he didn't realize he had shifted, stepping back into part of the narrow staircase that led backstage. When he felt someone bump into him from behind, he turned around, surprised.

"Excuse me," a tall, stout man whispered distractedly; he was bundled up in a roomy black overcoat, wearing a broad-brimmed hat and a white scarf.

"No, my fault, excuse *me*," don Pierino replied, hastily repairing to his niche. Worried about being discovered, he was afraid of causing problems for poor Patrisso. But the man didn't seem to think anything of his being there, and descending the remaining steps, headed for the dressing rooms. Don Pierino followed him with his eyes: was it possible that he was . . . In fact, the man, glancing around, paused a moment outside the door bearing a plaque which read: *Arnaldo Vezzi*. He said something and slipped into the dressing room. The priest nearly fainted: he had bumped into the greatest tenor on the planet! He sighed, and smiling, turned his attention back to the stage, where Turiddu was proposing a toast, extolling the praises of unadulterated wine.

The dressing room was cold, Ricciardi noted that right away. He looked toward the window and realized that it was partly open, letting in blasts of wintry wind and the scent of damp grass from the Royal Gardens. The bulbs over the mirror were lit, flooding the small room with light. There was blood everywhere. The corpse was on the chair in front of the mirror, bent over the dressing table, his back to the door. The mirror was completely shattered, except for the upper part that was spattered with blood. Glass was all over the place.

The body's head lay on the tabletop, resting on the left

cheek; on the right, a large fragment of mirror jutted out from the throat, reflecting a vitreous eye and a twisted mouth from which a trickle of drool oozed. Ricciardi heard singing in a soft voice:

"*Io sangue voglio, all'ira m'abbandono, in odio tutto l'amor mio finì . . .* ", I will have vengeance, My rage shall know no bounds, And all my love. Shall end in hate.

On the visible side of the face, the thick layer of grease paint was lined with the trace of a tear. The Commissario turned and, in the corner between the shattered mirror's frame and the wall, saw the image of Arnaldo Vezzi standing up, slightly bent at the knees, his face covered with make-up, his clown's mouth laughing. Fake tears drawn on his eyes, real tears down his cheeks. The right hand, palm open, stretched out as if to push someone away, and thick streams of blood pumped out by his dying heart through the gash on the right side of his neck. Ricciardi studied the ghost, taking his time: the lifeless eyes stared ahead without seeing him, the lips mouthed the lyrics and the chest no longer moved. The Commissario took one last look at the corpse. The clown's final song, just for him, and he didn't even understand opera. He turned towards the door and went out.

# VII

Don Pierino, entranced, watched the audience give a standing ovation to the troupe who had just concluded *Cavalleria Rusticana*. He was particularly proud, since he had seen the rehearsals the day before—using his usual mode of entry—and had grown fond of the singers. There were no prima donnas, only talented young people and some unassuming, easy-going professionals. A certain team spirit could be felt among them and it was pleasant to see how their camaraderie and mutual respect had generated the evening's success.

For the most part, the company was made up of local artists and served to fill in the 'gaps' that the season sometimes experienced due to illness or injuries on the part of the established players. Once they had rehearsed *La Traviata* in a week, due to the cancellation of *Swan Lake* when the prima ballerina sprained her ankle. But this time, don Pierino thought, they had really outdone themselves.

As he was enjoying the second call for the entire cast—the performers all holding hands and bowing to the public—he heard a woman's shrill scream behind him, coming from the dressing rooms.

The priest was used to hearing emotional outbursts in the cool darkness of the confessional, and his long-time passion as an opera-goer had trained his ear to the tones associated with different moods. He had no doubt or difficulty recognizing the horror, the shock. He turned and rushed towards the scream, his heart in his mouth. A small crowd was already gathering in front of Vezzi's dressing room.

Ricciardi looked around and spoke without addressing anyone in particular.

"I'm going into that office now," he said indicating the stage manager's small room, "and one by one Brigadier Maione will admit those I tell him. No one can go home, no one can leave the theater. No one can enter this dressing room, unless he's called in. You can't stay here, you must go somewhere else . . ." He thought for a moment. Yes. "On the stage. You will all gather on the stage, until we have finished. For the rest, clear the theater of everyone who could not have had access to this area: the public, the entrance staff. The police, however, will take everyone's information."

The theater director was purple with rage and rose up on his toes, sputtering.

"Such an affront . . . it's . . . it's unthinkable. Access to this area of the theater is highly restricted and selective. Moreover . . . do you realize who was in the audience tonight? And you want them to record information from the prefect, the nobility, the hierarchies . . . I demand, I insist that you respect the roles."

"My role is to reveal a murderer. Yours, sir, under these circumstances, is to facilitate my operation. Any other stance would constitute a crime, and would be prosecuted. Act accordingly."

Ricciardi's voice was a hiss, his green gaze was fixed on the director's face without batting an eye. The little man seemed to deflate, his heels settling on the floor in silence. He lowered his eyes and muttered: "I'll see to it at once. But I will speak out in the appropriate venues."

"Do whatever you like. Now go."

Stiffly, trying for some trace of his lost dignity, the director turned and walked towards the stage, followed by those present and their murmured comments.

The stage manager's office was tiny, almost entirely filled by a desk that held disorderly piles of drawings, notes and pages of scripts annotated by hand. On the walls, posters of performances. Two chairs stood in front of the desk, one behind. Light and air came from a small window high above. The first person Ricciardi spoke to was the stage manager himself, Giuseppe Lasio, the rumpled man who had broken down the door to Vezzi's dressing room.

"What exactly is your role?"

"I'm in charge of the staging. Virtually everything that has to do with the stage is under my direction. The lighting technicians, the actors' entrances and exits, the fixtures and equipment. Everything that isn't artistic; organizational support, in a word."

"What happened tonight? Tell me everything, please: even details that you think are insignificant."

Lasio frowned under his mop of red hair.

"It was after the intermezzo of *Cavalleria*, we were handling the exit after the toast. It's a choral scene, the entire company is onstage. The set was ready, the backdrop was in place. Signora Lilla came to call me at the stage entrance."

"Signora Lilla?"

"Letteria Galante, but we call her Signora Lilla. She's in charge of the theater's wardrobe department, for the principal actors she delivers the costumes directly. You've seen her, she's that . . . large woman. Sicilian. Very, very capable. Anyway, she came and told me: 'Sir, Vezzi isn't opening the door. We knocked, we called, but he doesn't answer.'"

"We?"

"Yes, she was with a young woman from wardrobe. There are thirty of them, I don't know them all. They were bringing his Canio costume, the clown outfit that you yourself later saw the girl holding. I rushed down, in a hurry, there's not a very long break between the end of *Cavalleria* and the beginning of *Pagliacci*, and Vezzi is . . . was . . . not always—how shall I put it?—precise and punctual. Sometimes he disappeared and we had to go looking around the theater for him, or even outside. He was one of the greats, you know: the greatest of all, onstage. But offstage, at times, he was difficult to manage. The kind who do whatever they like, and everyone else has to adapt. The privileges of talent."

"And did he go out tonight? Did you see him go out?"

"No, not me. But I'm always on the go, so he could have escaped my notice. In any case, I went down to the dressing room and I realized that the door was locked. That never happens. The singers, Vezzi especially, don't get up to open the door when they're putting on their make-up. I was worried."

"So what did you do?"

"After calling out to him myself, I thought Vezzi might not be feeling well so I kicked down the door. I was in the war, I'm used to seeing certain things. But I had never seen so much blood all at once. Signora Lilla came in behind me and screamed. Then everyone started running back and forth. I grabbed a stagehand and had him call you. Did I do the right thing?"

"Of course. After you, did anyone else enter the dressing room?"

"No. Definitely not. I myself waited by the door until you came. I was in the army, I told you. I know how things should be done."

"One last thing. The dressing-room door was locked, we said. But I haven't seen the key, either on the inside or on the outside. Did you remove it?"

Lasio ran his hands through his red hair, rumpling it even more, as he tried to remember.

"No, Commissario. The key wasn't there, either inside or outside, come to think of it."

"Thank you. You can leave the room, but don't go away. I might need additional information. Maione, send in the two seamstresses."

Signora Lilla sailed into the room like an ocean liner, filling the office. She was blonde, with piercing blue eyes. Behind her was the young woman, who by contrast seemed even smaller and thinner, wearing a smock at least one size too big. The large woman crossed her arms and looked at Ricciardi belligerently. "What do you mean, 'No one can leave the theater'? What do you think, that it was us? Look, all of us are here to work, we don't come here to do such awful things. We're decent people."

"No one is saying anything. Sit down and answer my questions. Tell me what happened."

Heaving a sigh, the woman sat down heavily, as though having made her preliminary remarks, a weight had been lifted off her chest and she could now speak more politely. Or maybe it was because the Commissario's determination, flashing out of those green eyes, brooked no opposition.

"We bring them down beforehand, the costumes. Long before. The normal singers try them on, ask for adjustments if needed, and that's that. Him, instead . . . he wants twenty fittings. First it's too short, then it's too long. Too loose, too tight. The collar button doesn't close. A real cross to bear. We're on the fourth floor, *Commissa'*. If you'll do us the honor, you'll see for yourself how things are up there, thirty of us. In the summer, it's so hot you can't breathe, what with the charcoal for the irons, and pedalling those sewing machines. Not even the coolness of the gardens gets up there. In the winter, on the other hand, we have to sew with gloves that leave the lower ends of our fingers bare, and even with all the stoves, we're covered with chilblains. But we don't complain, right Maddale"—she turned to the girl—"because work is work and we do our job well. The San Carlo is famous throughout the world, for its costumes as well, and we are its costumes. Still, when Vezzi is here we're constantly running up and down. Four flights of stairs, carrying pieces of fabric. But, God willing, the clown outfit was finally ready, down to the last adjustment made this very evening. I wanted to come down myself, with Maddalena here, to see if it suited him this time. And we found the door locked."

Ricciardi was thinking that he wouldn't have wanted to be in the tenor's place, if the costume had needed further modifications. Then, remembering Vezzi's current condition, he realized that his concern was pointless.

"What did you do when you realized the door was locked?"

"We called the stage manager, Lasio, to see what we should do. Otherwise we would have been blamed if the performance began late. He came and we waited outside the door."

"And him?"

"He knocked, he called out, then he kicked the door down. Now that's a man!" she said, suddenly coquettish. Ricciardi was stunned by the change. "Then I looked in and saw . . . it looked like the *mattanza*, the tuna slaughtering, in my village . . . I ran out. And that was it."

"And you, Signorina . . . ?"

"Maddalena Esposito at your service, *Commissa'*."

In further contrast to Signora Lilla, the young woman spoke softly, her eyes lowered. Neat and clean in her blue smock, her hands folded calmly in front of her, she was steady on her legs, though quite pale.

"Do you confirm everything?"

"Yes, sir, *Commissa'*. The Maestro was never satisfied; we adjusted his costume a number of times. Then I went down with Signora Lilla and the door was closed. I don't know what else I can tell you."

"All right. You may go. Maione, has the photographer arrived?"

# VIII

The police investigation consisted of photographs of the corpse taken from various angles. Only afterwards was it possible to remove the evidence that would be preserved for future examination. Ricciardi insisted on being present, to study the crime scene one last time and to make certain that in the turmoil of gathering evidence, no detail was altered, no indication that might be essential to his work. So when he left the stage manager's office, he found the photographer, the police technician and the coroner standing there sweating in their overcoats, waiting to be able to enter the dressing room. Acknowledging them with a nod, he went back inside to face the mirror fragments, the corpse and the tenor's image.

The chill in the dressing room had grown even sharper as the evening grew damper and cold air kept flowing in through the partly open window.

Ricciardi leaned out, noting that there was a flower bed no more than six feet below, in the gardens of the Royal Palace. Incredible how going up and down the stairs in the theater made you lose all sense of what floor you were on. Ducking back in, he was blinded by the flash of a camera. He rubbed his eyes, seeing clearly only the image of the tenor who kept repeating his lines. He knew very well that it wasn't his eyes that allowed him to see that vision. Once he was able to focus again, he noticed a detail that he had missed earlier: on the low sofa, beside the unhinged door, was a black overcoat with a broad-brimmed hat. On the floor, between the sofa and the corpse's feet, was a white wool scarf. Something wasn't right; what was it? It took Ricciardi a split second to figure it out: despite all that blood, lying right in the middle of a congealed puddle, the scarf was immaculate. Moving quickly, the Commissario picked the hat and coat up off the couch, revealing that the cushions underneath were soaked with the tenor's blood. All except one, with blue and white stripes, which was spotless.

The coroner was circling the body, making observations and jotting quick notes in a small notebook with a black cover. When the camera flashes stopped, he moved the body with the technician's help, transferring it on to the thick, blood-smeared carpet; the wool pullover that Vezzi had been wearing at the time of his death was completely saturated. How much blood could there be in the human body? And how much soul, Ricciardi thought, listening to the clown's song as he stood in the corner with his upraised hand. Which will disappear first, this stain on the carpet, or the echo of that aria in my head?

The medical examiner was a serious, conscientious professional whom Ricciardi had valued on other occasions. A fifty-year-old man, he had gained substantial experience in the war, in the Veneto: he had been on the Carso, between 1916 and 1918, and had also been decorated. His name was Bruno Modo, and he was one of the rare few whom Ricciardi addressed informally.

"So, Bruno? What can you tell me?"

"Let's see: puncture wound, slashed carotid artery. Bled to death, on this point there's no doubt. On the other hand . . . " He indicated the surroundings with a sweeping gesture. "A small ecchymosis under his left eye, on the cheekbone. One blow, maybe a punch. At first glance, nothing else: I see no other traumas, no skin under the nails . . . no marks on the knuckles . . . no tears on the scalp . . . " As he spoke he moved around the corpse stretched out on the floor and observed it through glasses perched on the tip of his nose. Occasionally he lifted one of the hands or brushed aside the hair. Delicately, though, with respect. That's why Ricciardi liked the man.

"When, do you think?"

"Oh, not long ago. A couple of hours, I'd say, maybe even less. But I'll be able to tell you more later, at the hospital."

Later, at the hospital. When all that's left of you, Ricciardi thought, looking at the body, will be bits and pieces sewn together somehow and the lines of an opera aria sung in the dark. No more complaining about your costume. The next one, your last, will be sewn on you without regard.

"Listen, Bruno. Could the weapon be a shard from the mirror?"

"I wouldn't say weapon. Seems to me it would be impossible to wield such a sharp piece of glass without cutting yourself, and I don't see traces of blood on the possible handhold. I'm leaning more toward the opinion that he fell on it, bodily. See how thick and pointed it is. It just might fit the facts: he takes a punch and ends up in the mirror. He's a big guy, look how heavy he is, tall and corpulent."

Maione interjected respectfully. "Doc, can you tell how he crashed into it? I mean, can you by chance see how he ended up in the mirror?"

"No, Brigadier. I don't see any other bruising. But it doesn't mean anything; he could have shoved it with his elbow, his shoulder. He was wearing a heavy wool pullover, it could have cushioned the blow. Then he fell on the chair and bled out. It doesn't take much with this type of wound: a matter of seconds. Look around, the room is inundated."

Ricciardi glanced briefly at the image of the tenor, his knees slightly bent and his hand raised. Is that the hand you broke the mirror with? And what are you crying for? Aren't you a clown?

"All right, if you're done here, let's move to the stage."

Ricciardi and Maione's arrival was greeted by a chorus; it was the right place for it after all, though the chorus was one of vehement protests. Some wanted to know if they were under arrest, others complained that their family was waiting, some were hungry, some cold. Everyone wanted to know why they were still being held. Ricciardi slowly raised a hand and there was silence.

"Settle down. I'll send you home soon. First I have to see you, I have to figure out who you are. All those who perform onstage, move to the right. Staff, technicians and orchestra members, to the left."

There was momentary confusion: it was an unscripted choreography. Some jostling, a little irritated grumbling, and two large groups were formed. Three, actually: left standing in the middle was a man dressed as a priest.

"And you? Make up your mind. Aren't you wearing a stage costume?"

"Well, you see, Commissario, it's not a costume . . . I'm don Pietro Fava, Assistant Pastor of San Ferdinando."

"And what are you doing here? The victim was already dead when they found him. Who called you?"

"No, no, Commissario, I . . . well, to tell the truth, I sneaked in."

There was general laughter, somewhat nervous. The stage manager stepped forwards, running his hand through his thick red hair.

"Commissario, I can explain, if you'll allow me."

"Please do."

"Don Pierino here is an old friend, you might say. He's an opera lover, a great fan. He thinks no one knows about it, but for two years now, with my permission, Patrisso, the gardens' caretaker, has been letting him in. He doesn't bother anybody, he stands on the landing of the narrow staircase and watches. We're used to seeing him, without him it feels like something is missing. The singers, the orchestra players consider him a lucky charm."

A murmur of assent and numerous smiles confirmed the stage manager's words. Don Pierino, alone in the centre of his beloved stage, blushed with pride, surprise and embarrassment.

"So," Ricciardi said, "you know opera, right? And also the theater. But you're neither a singer, nor an orchestra player, and you don't even work here. You know everybody, but you don't know anybody. Good."

Then he addressed the others.

"Right, the policemen have taken your information: you must not leave the city for the next few days. If someone needs to leave town, he must come to the Questura and tell us. If someone moves from one house to another, he must come to the Questura and tell us. If someone has anything to report, if he's remembered something, he should come to the Questura and tell us. For now, you can go. Not you, Father. I have to speak to you a moment."

With a choral sigh of relief, people crowded towards the exit. Only don Pierino was left standing where he was, now looking distressed and anxious. Not that he had anything to fear, but, he thought, the times were such that having anything to do with the police was never a good thing. Then too, he was genuinely saddened by Vezzi's death. He thought yearningly of the tenor's voice, that exquisite proof of God's love for man, that gift to opera lovers that he would never hear again except through the scratchy gramophone he kept in his little room.

## IX

The Commissario went over to him, followed, as usual, by the Brigadier, the older man two steps behind. Don Pierino had noticed that the burly officer virtually never took his eyes off his superior for a moment, and was constantly looking around, as though to assure himself that no danger was lurking. He must be very fond of him, he thought.

Ricciardi instead gave him a strange feeling. Seen from a distance, he was a man without any marked features: medium height, medium build, medium-priced clothing. But don Pierino had seen his eyes, when the Commissario arrived at the crime scene. And those eyes . . . those eyes had told him a great deal. Don Pierino, used to searching out and finding the truth behind an expression, had had the impression that he was looking at a multifaceted panorama. There was sorrow: an old sorrow, yet still alive. A sorrow that was an old friend. Loneliness. Intelligence, and a touch of irony, of sarcasm, when the theater director was sputtering beside him. It had only been a moment, but the priest had sensed a complex and troubled personality.

Now he stood in front of him: no hat, a few strands of black hair falling over his sharp nose. Hands in the pockets of his overcoat, which he had not taken off despite the heat. And then the eyes: green, almost transparent. He never blinked, and he wore a slight frown. Loneliness and sorrow, but also irony.

"So, Father: out of your territory tonight?"

"Why, does a priest have territorial limits? I've never seen a territory which couldn't use a priest. No, tonight I was off duty, if that's what you want to know. But I was still in uniform, as you can see."

Ricciardi twisted his face into what was meant to be a smile and lowered his eyes for a second. When he looked up again his forehead was smooth, but his expression hadn't changed.

"Certain uniforms, whether you wear them or don't wear them, it's all the same: you always have them on. You, me. Always with our uniforms on."

"The important thing is not to frighten people, with a uniform. People should feel reassured seeing it. And in order not to frighten people, you have to not be frightened."

The Commissario gave a faint start, as if the priest had suddenly slapped him. He tilted his head slightly to the side and stared at him with new regard. Behind him, two steps back, Maione shifted his weight from one foot to the other. The theater, now empty, listened in silence.

"And you, Father? Aren't you ever frightened?"

"Yes, almost always. But I ask for help. From the Almighty, from people. And I get over it."

"Bravo, Father. Bravo. Good for you. Now, let's get to the . . . 'dolesome notes', I believe they say. This is the right place for it. So then, you know opera, and this setting. You can help me, since I don't know either one. Would you make a deal, with a policeman?"

Sarcasm again. No smile, no wink. The unchanging green glass of his eyes.

"A priest doesn't make deals, Commissario. He has no choice when it comes to the seal of the confessional. And he does not inform. He doesn't blow the whistle on some poor devil."

"Oh, I see. Better that a poor devil should go to jail, perhaps by omission. And that the true perpetrator remain on the streets, to commit another crime. You're right, Father. It means I'll have to look elsewhere for help."

Maione was surprised: he had rarely heard Ricciardi say so much. He hadn't really understood the conversation, but he sensed that the Commissario had grown even more disheartened. He could tell by the stiffening of his back, by the way he held his head. The little priest, who looked so cool and composed, rocking on his toes with his hands clasped over his stomach, was giving him a hard time. Like a hunting dog eager to follow the prey's scent, the Brigadier felt that they were just wasting time. However, his brother-in-law was at his house and he wasn't eager to go home.

"No, Commissario," don Pierino said, "that's not what I meant. Naturally, I will give you any information you need; but don't ask me, now or later, to help you accuse someone. Yours is human justice. I deal with another justice: one that can also forgive."

"I won't encroach on your territory, Father. I wouldn't let you encroach on mine. I'll expect you at the Questura tomorrow morning at eight, in my office. Please don't be late."

Without waiting for a response, he turned and walked away. Maione looked at the priest thoughtfully for a moment, then followed Ricciardi out of the theater.

Despite the fact that it was now eleven o'clock and that he had come out by the side door, Ricciardi found a swarm of journalists and curious bystanders waiting for him, heedless of the raging wind that whistled through the portico. Maione stepped in front and firmly pushed aside those who pressed the Commissario, trying to snatch a comment for the next edition of their papers. Ricciardi didn't so much as look up; he was used to ignoring the living and the dead who called out to him, even though he always heard them.

During the short walk to the Questura, the two men did not exchange many words. Maione was quite clear on the course the investigation would take starting tomorrow: determining the victim's final hours and questioning possible witnesses. The Brigadier knew how the Commissario operated, that he looked for possible motives, circumstances, words that could put them on the right track, with maniacal attention to detail. The days would be exhausting. He hoped that by that hour his brother-in-law would be gone at least.

When they reached the Questura, Ricciardi nodded goodnight to Maione and began walking back up Via Toledo. His pace was swift, his head ducked, the wind at his back. The city, which in other seasons at that hour still rang with songs and voices calling out, was already silent that night. Scraps of newspaper swirled in the street, in the swaying patches of light cast by street lamps hung from power cables. His footsteps echoed on the paving stones, acting as counterpoint to the occasional howling of the wind in the recess of some shop or in the doorways of the old buildings. The dead man in Largo della Carità again informed him that he would not let the thief take his things, as he went on bleeding and oozing brain matter. Ricciardi did not bother to look at him.

He was thinking. An open window, given how cold it was, in the dressing room of a man who had to take care of his voice and be cautious about draughts—it didn't make sense. The spotless overcoat on the blood-stained sofa—it didn't make sense. The white scarf on the floor, immaculate—it didn't make sense. The striped cushion, the only one without a blood stain—it didn't make sense. The locked door—it didn't make sense. But what if all these things taken as a whole made sense? The boy on the corner of Via Salvator Rosa, with his poor mangled skeleton, asked him if he could go down and play. The image was beginning to fade, maybe it would disappear and he would be able to sleep peacefully. Ricciardi hoped it would happen soon.

He had reached his house.

# X

Rosa Vaglio was seventy years old. She was born the same year as Italy, but she took no notice of it, then or later. For her, the homeland had always been the Family, of which she was a staunch, resolute custodian. She had entered the household of Ricciardi di Malomonte when she was fourteen years old. She was the tenth of twelve children and the Baroness had chosen her without hesitation.

She remembered that day as if it were yesterday: the tall, blonde woman, smiling, negotiating the price with her father. She had been friends with the son, a little older than her, until he had gone off to study in Naples, where he remained for many years. Rosa had a keen intelligence and had soon become the person everyone turned to in the grand family villa in Fortino. After the death of the old Baron and that of the Baroness later on, she had kept things going as if they might return from a trip at any moment.

Instead it was the son, now forty, who came back with his child bride. As she busied herself in the kitchen, that evening of 25 March 1931, sighing over yet another delayed dinner, she gave a quick smile at the thought: her little girl. Actually, little lady Marta was already twenty years old. She looked just like a teenager though, petite, slim, dark-haired, eyes so green they bored into your soul. And all that sorrow.

Rosa had often wondered where that sorrow in the eyes of the young Baroness came from. She had everything she wanted, leisure, affluence, a loving husband. But when she accompanied her on long walks through Fortino's countryside, amid the pungent smell of goats and the peasants who stopped working to take off their hats, she felt that sorrow walking with them, one step behind. Perhaps it was memories, or regrets. Baroness Marta spoke little. But she smiled at Rosa, tenderly, and caressed her face sometimes, as if she herself were twenty years older.

Rosa remembered the morning of October 1899, the last year of the century, when they sat on a bench on the terrace, embroidering, and Marta had raised her green eyes to her and told her: "Rosa, starting tomorrow we have to sew sheets for a cradle." Just like that, simply. From that time on, she had become *tata* Rosa and would be so all her life.

"You know I don't want you to wait up for me. It's late for you, you should already be asleep."

Ricciardi felt the warmth of the house seep gradually into his wind-chilled bones. The scent of wood fire in the stove, the aromas from the kitchen: garlic, beans, oil. The lamp next to his armchair was lit, the newspaper on the armrest. In the bedroom, his flannel robe, soft leather slippers and hairnet. My *tata*, he thought.

"Oh sure: I go to sleep and let you go hungry. What do you think, I don't know that you would go to bed without eating? That you would always wear the same suit and the same shirt, if I didn't lay them out on the bed for you? It's not normal, thirty years old and no woman. Not to mention, given these times, it won't be long before they actually start arresting bachelors. With so many attractive young women out there. And you, you're handsome, rich, young, from a good family. What more could a woman want? That way you can put me in a rest home and begin to live for a change."

There: she'd said it. Sitting down at the table, he was very careful not to sigh. It would give rise to an endless tirade and he had an appointment for which he was already very late.

Rosa watched him eat, like a wolf, as usual. Bent over his plate, quick, silent mouthfuls. He denies himself even that, she thought, the pleasure of savouring. He never savoured anything, not food or anything else. In him, the sorrow that in his mother had been concealed became evident. The same green eyes. The same sorrow. She had cared for him all his life, through the feverish nights, the loneliness. All through his years at boarding school she had been there waiting for him, during vacations, holidays, Sundays, letting him find the things he liked without him asking her for them. She sensed the turmoil of his thoughts, though she didn't know what these thoughts were. She had been his family and he had become her reason for living. She would have given her eye teeth to see him laugh, at least once. She would have liked to see him at peace, not detached from others and from the quickly spinning world which he stood watching from a distance, hands in his pockets and a strand of hair over his face. Not smiling, not saying anything. And yet, what did he lack?

She was moved, a mother's concern. He seemed like a child again, lost in thought as he ate. He had always liked beans.

Ricciardi had never liked beans, but he would never disappoint his *tata*; besides he was hungry tonight, maybe because of the chill he felt in his bones. He thought again about the crime scene. If the coat and scarf had been brought into the dressing room after Vezzi's death, who had brought them? And why? The only ones who had admitted seeing the dressing room after the crime had been Lasio, the stage manager, the wardrobe mistress Lilla and the seamstress. Mopping up the sauce with his bread, Ricciardi recalled the large woman's enchanted expression in the presence of the stage manager: was it possible they were in cahoots? And the seamstress, that Esposito, was she in on it too? No, too many people. And too much blood. The murder had not been planned, he was certain of that. And the open window? And the small, striped cushion? So many questions and the Incident wasn't helping him. It happened frequently: what he heard from the victim's image could also be misleading, and could throw him off track. It was a feeling, a sensation, not a rationally framed message. Grief, rage, hatred, even love.

A glass of red wine, then another: after each new death he found it hard to sleep. The image stayed with him like a flutter in his chest, an expectancy. Maybe it was transmitting the fear of death to him, fear of the final moment. Fear of what? He thought about it. As long as you're alive, death doesn't exist; once death comes, you no longer exist. Still, you'll meet death, he had said to the Jesuit at the boarding school, at the age of seventeen. But afterwards you'll meet God, the Jesuit had replied.

Is there a God? Sipping his wine, Ricciardi thought about the strange priest he had met at the theater; his shrewd replies, sparkling eyes. He seemed like a good man. Another one who thought there was a God. Where was God for him, when he saw the image of sorrow and felt its reverberation? Was it up to him alone to relieve that sorrow?

Ricciardi got up from the table, otherwise his *tata* would stand there all night watching him drink, without clearing the dishes. He kissed her tenderly on the forehead and went to his bedroom to keep his appointment.

# XI

The blonde woman was walking along the walls of Piazza Carolina, heading up towards Via Gennaro Serra. The cold wind from the sea drove her along, but her steps were dragging. In contrast to the rare passers-by scurrying to reach the warmth of their homes, she had no desire to face those eyes that bore into her, searching out her hidden feelings.

She had become good at dissembling, at concealing. She had to prevent anyone from knowing, had to keep what had happened from becoming common knowledge. In the uncertain light of the street lamps, walking more and more slowly, she felt her lover's hands on her body; she recalled his face, his voice, the shallow breathing. She thought about the words that were said, the promises, the plans. How could it have happened? she wondered. And now, how could she hide it from her man's eyes, that she loved another man, that she dreamed of leaving with him?

She ran her hand over her face, under the hat that hid her beautiful eyes. Tears. She was crying. She had to compose herself, she wasn't far from home. She glimpsed the dark shape of the church of Santa Maria degli Angeli, at the top of Pizzofalcone hill. Soon she would have to face the man who loved her so much that he could read her thoughts. She was remorseful. She felt bad for him, for having betrayed him. She had to make sure no one found out, she had to protect him from scandal.

Quickening her pace, she wondered again what would happen.

Like every night, Ricciardi closed the door of his room behind him. Before going to bed he would open it a crack to hear his *tata* Rosa's heavy breathing and be reassured by its regularity. He changed into his robe, and put a hairnet over his hair. With the lights turned off, he went to the window and parted the curtains. The patch of sky, swept clear and cloudless by the strong north wind, displayed four bright stars; Ricciardi wanted to be illuminated, but not by the stars.

The light that mattered to him was that of a dim lamp on a small table, behind the window across from his in the building opposite. The table was beside an armchair in which a young woman sat, embroidering. A cosy corner in the large room that was the kitchen. Ricciardi knew that her name was Enrica and that she was the eldest of five children: a large family. The father was a hat merchant. One of Enrica's sisters, married and the mother of a young child, lived with her husband in the same apartment. The young woman was embroidering with her left hand, lost in thought. She wore tortoiseshell glasses. Ricciardi also knew that she bent her head a little when she was focusing; that her gestures were fluid and graceful, though she didn't know what to do with her hands when she talked; that she was left-handed; that she would suddenly laugh when playing with her siblings or her little nephew; and that sometimes she cried, when she was alone and thought no one could see her.

There wasn't a single night when he didn't spend some time at the window, experiencing Enrica's life vicariously. It was the only time he granted his tormented spirit a brief respite. He watched her at supper, serene and amiable with her family, seated to her mother's left. Listening to the radio, her expression intent and engrossed, or to a recording on the monumental gramophone, spellbound, with a hint of a smile. Reading with her head bowed, moistening a finger to turn the page. Arguing, softly but stubbornly speaking up for herself. He had never spoken to her, but there was no one, surely, who knew her better than he did.

Indeed, he had never exchanged a word with her, nor did he think that would ever happen. One Sunday, when his *tata* wasn't able to, he had gone to buy vegetables from the street vendor who came down from Capodimonte. He had paid, turned around with a bunch of broccoli under his arm, and there she was in front of him, face to face. He still shuddered at the memory of the extraordinary mixture of pleasure, awkwardness, joy and terror he had felt. Afterwards, in the drowsy state that preceded sleep, or at the moments when he woke up, he would see those deep, dark eyes hundreds of times. That day he had fled, his heart leaping in his chest, a loud pounding in his ears. Not turning around, dropping bits of broccoli along the way, his eyes half-closed to retain the image of those long legs and that faint smile that he had perhaps glimpsed. How could I speak to you? What could I offer you, except the distress of seeing me perpetually worn out?

In the small cone of lamplight, Enrica went on embroidering, unaware.

Before giving in to sleep, Ricciardi thought again about the clown and his desperate last song.

"*Io sangue voglio, all'ira m'abbandono, in odio tutto l'amor mio finì . . .* " I will have vengeance . . . , and all my love shall end in hate.

What makes a man at the point of death sing? Was he getting ready to go onstage? Rehearsing his role? Why was he crying? Ricciardi clearly recalled the streak the tear had left on the white greasepaint. Or maybe the tears expressed an emotion related to the opera? And if so, what? What was unique about this performance? Why was the protagonist still in his dressing room putting on make-up while they had been singing for over an hour onstage? He had to learn more about it. He had to enter Vezzi's life and his curious profession made up of fiction and make-believe. He would ask the priest for help.

And as the wind rattled the shutters, Ricciardi drifted into a muddled dream in which a left-handed girl embroidered in front of a weeping clown.

# XII

The following morning, the wintry wind had not lost its intensity. Heavy dark clouds raced across the sky, allowing the sun's rays to light up bits of the city at intervals, as if they were spotlights focused haphazardly to capture even the most insignificant details. On his way to the Questura, Ricciardi saw men chasing their hats, barefoot children racing in the wind, their hand-me-down shirts billowing like sails, heedless of the cold, and beggars huddling in tattered rags, seeking refuge in building doorways only to be chased away by intolerant porters.

Ricciardi thought about how much the city might change, as times themselves changed. In the frigid wind and fickle light, the old buildings teeming with life became dark caves and new construction sites seemed like monuments to loneliness and neglect.

When he got to the office, he found Vice Questore Garzo's clerk waiting for him at the door; Garzo was Ricciardi's boss. The small man, partly because of the cold, and partly because of his obvious state of anxiety, was stamping his feet softly on the ground and rubbing his hands together.

"Ah, Commissario Ricciardi. Finally, I've been freezing, such a wind . . . The Vice Questore would like to see you in his office, immediately."

The clerk's name was Ponte. He was one of those who felt uneasy in the Commissario's presence and had a superstitious dread of him. He always avoided making eye contact with him or getting in his way. Even on this occasion his eyes kept shifting, looking down at the floor a little, then up at the ceiling, a little to the side, with an occasional darting glance at his interlocutor. Ricciardi was annoyed with him, both because he suspected the reason for the man's agitation, and because he found it hard to tell from his expression what it was all about.

"At this hour? Usually I'm the only one up here on this floor until ten. All right. I'll take off my coat and I'm on my way."

"No, sir, please: the Vice Questore said, 'I want him in my office immediately.' He's been here since seven thirty! Please, sir. He'll take it out on me!"

"I said I want to take off my coat first. You'll just have to wait, you and the Vice Questore. Please step aside."

Given that biting tone and harsh look, Ponte moved aside with a little leap, although it was clear he was acutely uneasy. Ricciardi went into the office, taking his time, hung his coat in the dark wood armoire, smoothed his hair back and followed the agitated clerk down the hall.

Angelo Garzo was an ambitious hustler. His entire life, not just his career, was marked by a driving ambition. About to turn forty, he was champing at the bit to have a Questura assigned to him, even a minor one.

He felt he had all the requirements: good looks, excellent people skills, a perfect family, dedication to his work, Party membership and participation in political activities, an aptitude for pleasing his superiors and a firm hand with his subordinates. He considered himself endowed with excellent organizational abilities, he conscientiously and constantly showed his face everywhere, he was moderately social and, in his opinion, likable enough. But in reality he was inept.

The climb to his present position had from time to time been marked by betrayal, cunning, and servility towards his superiors. And above all by the skilful exploitation of his subordinates' capacities.

So it was in this spirit that he welcomed Ricciardi when the latter appeared at his door, accompanied by the clerk.

"My dear, dear Ricciardi! I was waiting anxiously for you! Please, come in." He had stepped around the desk, perfectly clear of any clutter except for a single sheet of paper, placed squarely in the centre. He glared at Ponte, hissing, "I told you *immediately*! Get out of here."

Ricciardi went in, taking a quick look around. Although similar in size to his own, Garzo's office had a very different appearance. It was very neat, and there were no stacks of reports or old file folders; a large bookcase behind the desk was full of austere volumes on laws and statutes, obviously never opened. On the wide back of the brown leather chair, where the head would rest, was a soft green cloth. In front of the desk, two dark red leather chairs, each with a small cushion. A large vase sat atop a low open cabinet, in which a crystal bottle and four *rosolio* glasses could be seen. On the walls, in addition to the two regulation portraits of Mussolini and the King, a standard letter of commendation given to the Questura of Avellino, which Garzo had unduly appropriated. On the desktop, as a final touch to the green leather desk pad and letter opener, the photograph of a woman, not beautiful but smiling, with two serious children dressed in sailor suits.

Of all that ostentatious display, Ricciardi envied only the photograph.

In the corridors it was whispered that Garzo's wife was the granddaughter of the Prefect of Salerno, and that much of his career depended on that marriage. Still, Ricciardi thought, in your life there's a smile. In mine, only a hand that embroiders, seen from too far away.

Garzo, with his persuasive, well-pitched voice, accompanied his words with fluid gestures.

"Please, come in. Have a seat. You see, Ricciardi, I'm well aware of what you may be thinking: that you lack the explicit praise of your superior, that your work is not always appreciated enough, that you don't get the recognition that you would like. I also know that, at the time of the splendid, swift resolution of the Carosino crime, you would have expected a commendation from the Questore, who instead chose the occasion to direct his applause to the entire mobile unit, speaking through my humble person. But, and this should always be kept firmly in mind, my esteem and my regard for you are never lacking. And if a positive situation were to develop, I would be able to prove to you with actions how much I appreciate your cooperation."

Ricciardi listened grimly, his hands in constant motion. He was aware of how false Garzo's words were, since the man considered him a threat to his position. The Vice Questore would gladly have gotten rid of that strange, silent man, his eyes like daggers: not a friend, never a familiar overture, and according to what they said he had no attachments or particular sexual inclinations that might make him more vulnerable. Unfortunately, he was very capable. Cases that seemed extremely complex, that he couldn't even read in their entirety, were solved by that individual with almost supernatural ability. As if what was whispered around were true: that he conversed with the devil himself, who told him about his transgressions. Garzo thought that, in order to understand crime so well, you had to be something of a criminal yourself. That was why he, a good person, could never figure it out.

"Why did you send for me?" Ricciardi cut him off.

Garzo seemed almost offended by the Commissario's brusque manner, but only for a moment. He quickly resumed his blandishments, in a conciliatory tone.

"Right, right, we have no time to lose. We're men of action. So then, last night at the San Carlo . . . I wasn't there, a work commitment that couldn't be put off. I too never have a moment to enjoy myself. I heard about your timely intervention. My compliments, you too at work at such a late hour. With your officer, Brigadier, what's his name . . . Maione, yes. How did it go? I heard you were a little . . . curt, as they say. Not that it isn't necessary at times, as I well know. But, damn it, the signor Prefect was there, Prince d'Avalos, the Colonnas, the Santa Severinas . . . Wasn't there some way to avoid taking their information? You, Ricciardi, are sometimes too . . . direct. I say this for your own good. You're very capable, you should be more diplomatic, at least with those who count. There have been complaints. Even from the theater director, Spinelli. A bit of a queen, but with important contacts."

Ricciardi hadn't moved a muscle. He had listened in silence, without batting an eye.

"Feel free to assign the case to someone else, sir. That's the way I work. In accordance with procedures, I believe."

"Oh, but of course! And I wouldn't even dream of handing over the case to anyone else. There is no one better able to solve this case. That's exactly why I sent for you so early. Where are we with it?"

"We'll begin this morning. We'll do another inspection of the crime scene, take the witnesses' testimony. We'll work non-stop."

"There, that's good: non-stop. I'll be frank with you, Ricciardi. This is something big, bigger than we can imagine. This singer . . . Vezzi . . . he was the best in his field, apparently. The fans adored him, a real source of national pride. And in times like these, when national pride is of absolute importance . . . It seems that *Il Duce* himself admired him and went to hear him, when he sang in Rome. They say he was as good and even better than Caruso himself. And the fact that what happened took place here in our city has filled the authorities with dismay. But let's be clear about it, it's also an opportunity. If we were to find the perpetrator with our usual speed and thoroughness, as you so often do, well, this would bring me . . . would bring us directly to the attention of the highest offices in the nation, Ricciardi. Do you understand that?"

"I understand that there's a man dead, sir. A murdered man; and a murderer who is walking freely about the city. As always, it will take whatever time it takes. And as always, we will do everything that can and must be done. Without losing any time. If we don't lose any time, that is."

This time Garzo could not help noticing the cold sarcasm in the Commissario's words.

"Look, Ricciardi," he said, frowning, "I have no intention of standing here and being disrespected. I called you in to tell you how important this investigation is, for your own good, first of all. As you know, I would not hesitate to ascribe the failure to you, if you should fail. I will not risk my career because of your mistakes. Do well and it will go well for everyone. Fall short and you will pay. You see this?" he said, pointing to the sheet of paper on his desk. "This transcribed phone message comes from the Minister of the Interior. It directs us to disclose every bit of progress in the investigation. The least bit of progress, do I make myself clear, Ricciardi? Keep me apprised, step by step. The signor Questore will in turn report to Rome. Anything else you're working on is on hold."

At last, Ricciardi recognized the real Garzo.

"As usual, sir. I will handle the matter as usual. With all due attention."

"I have no doubt, Ricciardi. I have no doubt. You can go."

Outside the door, the clerk Ponte carefully avoided looking at him.

# XIII

Don Pierino had said Mass at seven. He liked the early hour. The eyes of people who sought God before beginning another day's battle. At that hour there was no social distinction amid the pews; men and women dressed differently but shared the same impulse.

That morning, moreover, the weather was strange and beautiful: the wind howled fiercely through the narrow central nave and the light from the tall windows was sporadic, as if to say that it should not be considered a given, but something to be earned through effort, like the fruits of the earth and one's daily bread.

When the Mass was over, don Pierino put on his threadbare overcoat and, holding on to his hat with one hand, headed towards the nearby questura for his appointment with the Commissario. Since the night before, he had been thinking about that intense gaze and what he had seen in it.

Besides a natural concern for one's fellow man, the practice of the priesthood had added the ability to recognize the feelings that lay hidden behind expressions, behind the words dictated by circumstances; so that the little priest had learned to carry on two dialogues simultaneously, one with the mouth and one with the eyes. Offering help to those who needed it and could not find the strength to ask for it.

The Commissario's gaze, those formidable green eyes, were a window on the tempest within.

Don Pierino recalled that, just after taking his vows, he had attended to patients in an old hospital in Irpinia, where children suffering from contagious diseases were shut away in a separate room. The door to this ward had a window, and a child suffering from cholera was always glued to it. He had read a similar despair in the eyes of that child as he watched his more fortunate peers able to be together, playing. The small mark his breath left on the glass conveyed a sense of exclusion, of immense loneliness: being condemned to remain at the margins of other peoples' lives, without ever sharing them.

As he walked against the wind, the priest realized that all in all he didn't mind meeting the policeman, intrigued as he was by that desperate mind.

Ricciardi went to meet don Pierino at the door to his office. He shook the priest's hand—a brief, firm grip—making no attempt to kiss it. He had him sit down in front of the desk which, the Assistant Pastor noticed, held no photographs or any objects that might say something about the life of the man who worked there. Only a strange paperweight, a lump of blackened, half-melted iron, from which a stylized metal pen stuck out, as to pretty up the unsightly object.

"How strange," the priest said, stroking it briefly.

"A piece of shrapnel; it dates back to the war."

"Were you in the war?"

"No, I was too young. I was born in 1900. An old friend gave it to me. The grenade almost killed him and he wanted to preserve the memory. That's what they say, isn't it? What doesn't kill you makes you stronger."

"So they say, yes. But help also strengthens you. The help of others, of God."

"When it's there, Father. When it's there. So then, what can you tell me about yesterday? Have you given it some thought? Do you have any idea of what might have happened? Who might have done it?"

"No, Commissario. I could never come up with an idea like that, not even if I wanted to identify with the individual and, believe me, I don't. Then, too, a voice like that! How can one even think of snuffing it out forever? A gift to us all, straight from God Almighty."

"Why, Father? Was this Vezzi all that great?"

"Not great. Celestial. I like to think that the angels have voices like Vezzi's, to sing the praises of the Lord in heaven. If that were so, no one would be afraid of dying. I heard him twice, in Verdi's *Il Trovatore* and Donizetti's *Lucia di Lammermoor*; he, of course, was Manrico in the first and Edgardo in the second. You should have heard him, Commissario. He plucked your heart out of your chest, took it to heaven, bathed it in the moon and stars, and returned it to you shining and renewed. When he finished singing I saw that my face was wet with tears; and I hadn't realized I was crying. Seeing him up close, yesterday, made my heart tremble."

Ricciardi listened to the priest, staring at him over hands joined together in front of his mouth. He sensed his childlike enthusiasm and wondered how opera, mere make-believe, could produce such emotion. He also felt a little envious, because he himself had never experienced such a profound, indulgent frame of mind.

"And this time, how did he sing?"

"No, Commissario, this time he had not yet sung. It was opening night, yesterday: the night of the première. And he hadn't been onstage yet."

"So how come the performance was already underway? Who was singing, at the time?"

"Oh, I understand your confusion. I should explain. Well then, generally only one opera is performed, in three or more acts. In this case, however, since these are short works, two of them are performed: Mascagni's *Cavalleria Rusticana* and Leoncavallo's *Pagliacci*. They are two operas that date back to the same period, the first is from 1890 and the second from 1892, I believe."

"And Vezzi only sang in one of the two?"

"That's right, in *Pagliacci*. He plays . . . he would have played Canio, the lead role. A difficult part, I read that he was even greater than usual in it."

"It was the second opera, then."

"Yes, very good, the second. That's how they are usually performed: first *Cavalleria* and then *Pagliacci*, which is more compelling and vivid, so the audience's attention is more easily captured. Personally, from a musical standpoint I prefer *Cavalleria*, which has an extraordinary intermezzo. But there are several beautiful arias in *Pagliacci*, specifically in Canio's role. Vezzi would never have played Turiddu in *Cavalleria*, for example."

Ricciardi listened very carefully. He absorbed the information voraciously, reflecting on the situations that might have arisen the night of the murder.

"But aside from the principal roles, the singers are the same?"

"They could be, but generally that's not the case. In this instance, Vezzi had a cast put together specifically for him; whereas *Cavalleria* was performed by a troupe that appears frequently at the San Carlo. Normally they are so-so, middling to average, but this time they were really very good. It was a splendid surprise. Even though this aspect later became of secondary importance, unfortunately. The evening will certainly not be remembered for the performance."

"So the rehearsals are separate? The troupes never come into contact with one another?"

"No, apart from some orchestra rehearsals, in which individual openings and a few scenes are practised and repeated, it is unlikely that the two companies will overlap. Even during the shows, like last night, there is sufficient time between the two performances for the turnover to occur without contact. Naturally, many of the singers know one another. They work in the same theater, after all."

"And the orchestra. The orchestra is shared, isn't it?"

"Of course, the orchestra is the same. It's associated with the theater, along with its conductor, Maestro Mariano Pelosi: a gentleman, as well as a professional. In his day it seemed he would have a brilliant career, that he would be another Toscanini. Then it stalled. But he's a more than reputable conductor and the San Carlo is one of the greatest opera houses in the world."

"And the two operas? Tell me something about their story lines."

"Well, the two operas . . . Their themes are similar, though treated differently. *Cavalleria Rusticana* is based on Verga, set in Sicily on Easter morning. It has only one act, with the intermezzo I mentioned. There is a young man, Turiddu, a tenor, who is engaged to Santuzza but still loves Lola, his former girlfriend. She, however, is married to the wagoner Alfio, a baritone. In short, two couples, one old love story and two new ones. Santuzza, distraught and jealous, tells Alfio about Turiddu and Lola and, in a final duel, Alfio kills Turiddu. The female roles in this opera are the best parts, in my opinion: Lola, Santuzza and Lucia, Turiddu's mother.

'*Pagliacci*, on the other hand, takes place in Calabria. It runs as long as *Cavalleria*, more or less. A troupe of actors arrive in a little village: the head of the company is Canio, the tenor, who was to be played by Vezzi. He is a man who is anything but jovial, despite his role as a clown; in reality he is poisoned by jealousy over his wife Nedda, who plays Colombina, when they perform. In fact, Nedda cheats on him with Silvio, a wealthy young man who lives in the village. In the end, in a very beautiful, dramatic scene, we go from fiction to reality and Canio, Pagliaccio, tearing off his costume, kills both Nedda and her lover. The beauty of the opera, aside from the music, is the mingling of reality and performance: the audience can't tell if the singers are playacting or acting for real, until blood flows.

"As you can see, Commissario, the themes are the same: jealousy, love and death. Just as, unfortunately, we often find in everyday life as well, wouldn't you say?"

"Maybe, Father. But perhaps everyday life has other complications. There's hunger, for example. Is hunger ever found in your operas? If you knew how much hunger there is, in crimes, Father. But let's get back to Vezzi. As far as you know, what was Vezzi like in real life? Was he well liked?"

"I couldn't say. Generally, when I can—thanks to the kindness of my parishioner Patrisso who is the caretaker at the gardens entrance—I like to attend the rehearsals, especially the dress rehearsals, which are in costume. But this time, for Pagliacci, they held the rehearsal behind tightly closed doors. There's a great deal of attention surrounding Vezzi: they say he's actually Mussolini's favourite tenor."

"Yes, so I've heard. All right, Father. Thank you very much. If I need any further information, may I trouble you again? As I said before, you know I don't know much about these things."

"Certainly, Commissario. But let me say one thing: it wouldn't hurt, maybe, if you were to listen to some opera. It would do you good to see how beautiful a feeling, its expression, can be."

Surprisingly, don Pierino saw a shadow of immense sorrow in Ricciardi's green eyes. Not a recollection but rather a condition. As if, just for a moment, the policeman had opened a window on the mysterious territory of his soul.

"I know about feelings, Father. And one can also have too much of them. Thank you. You may go."

At the door, don Pierino ran into Maione who was on his way in.

"Good morning, Father. Have you already given your opera lesson?"

"Good morning to you, Brigadier. I provided some information, yes. But I don't think the Commissario will ever be a regular attendee at the San Carlo. If you need me, I'll be at the church."

Maione sat down after giving Ricciardi a sketchy military salute.

"So then, *Commissa'*: we picked up last night's depositions. This is the list of those who were onstage for *Cavalleria Rusticana* as well as members of the orchestra. Dr. Modo, who is expecting us at the hospital this morning but not before noon, has already said that Vezzi could not have died prior to an hour before he was found, therefore the first opera was already underway. This would exclude both the singers of *Cavalleria* and the musicians, wouldn't it? How could they have moved during the opera? This instead is a list of the cast of Pagliacci, whom I think we should check carefully."

"Everything should be checked carefully. The staff?"

"As we've seen, there weren't very many of them who had access to the dressing rooms. It's generally a restricted area to begin with, then when Vezzi comes, the doorman told me, the place is treated like a deluxe hotel. It seems that when anyone appeared at the doorman's station, Vezzi demanded that he personally be asked whether the individual could be let in. So we can eliminate from consideration the staff who would normally be admitted."

Ricciardi knew that Maione had thoroughly verified the information before presenting it to him, and that he could trust the report.

"Who will we find this morning at the San Carlo?"

"The theater director, for sure. The man seems to have lost his senses, yesterday he was hopping up and down, snivelling and whining, making a huge pest of himself. He was angry with you, he said he'd have them take you off the investigation. Then, the orchestra members: I've been told they have to rehearse every day, it's a contractual matter. We only closed off the area of the dressing rooms, the section of the Royal Palace gardens under the windows and the side entrance, so they can work between the stage and the concert hall. Also, Vezzi's people phoned, his manager, a certain Marelli, from up north, calling on behalf of his wife, a former singer from Pesaro, Livia Lucani. They wanted to know when they could reclaim the corpse for the funeral. I told them to call back later. However, they are coming to Naples, they've been travelling since last night, and they'll arrive at the station this evening."

"As soon as they get here I want to talk to them. Now, let's get to the theater."

# XIV

Garzo's clerk, Ponte, stood in the office corridor, chilly as usual. He stepped forward as soon as he saw Ricciardi and Maione.

"Sir, the Vice Questore wanted . . . if you could stop by a moment . . . "

"No, I can't. When I get back, maybe. I'm pursuing the investigation, without losing any time: according to his orders. Give him my regards."

They hurried off down the stairs, leaving the little man frozen in more ways than one since he would now have to face the Vice Questore's wrath by himself.

Ricciardi had no intention of wasting precious hours. He was well aware that solutions resulting from the investigations were a race against time, where the odds of success diminished with the passing of just a few minutes. An old commissario with whom he had worked maintained that forty-eight hours after the crime the murderer will no longer be found, unless he turns himself in. And this only happened on the rare occasions when the voice of conscience became deafening and plunged the killer's soul straight to hell. More often, much more often, what prevailed was the desire to avoid hell on earth, namely the punishment of men.

He recalled a prior offender arrested for theft a couple of years ago: after submitting to being held and remaining silent until then, the man had seized the gun of one of the two policemen who were escorting him and, without hesitation, right there in the courtyard of the Questura, fired a shot at his temple, killing the guard on his opposite side with the same bullet.

For months, Ricciardi had seen the two of them in the corner of the courtyard: the prisoner kept yelling that he would not go back to that hellhole of a prison, the policeman called out to his wife and son. Both men had a big hole in the right temple, and brain matter mixed with black blood oozed from the bullet wound.

Outside, the city was a whirlwind. Violent gusts kept pedestrians from crossing the exposed spaces of streets or piazzas, so everyone made their way along by hugging the walls. The heavy trams seemed to sway on the rails, shaken by the strong blasts, and the coachmen of the few carriages were bent over the seat, the whip gripped tightly in their hands. In the air, the scent of wood smoke from stoves and the smell of horse manure was revived with every gust. The foliage of the trees that lined the streets tossed and swirled, broken branches and broad green leaves rose and fell, in imitation of an autumn that was still far off.

Ricciardi and Maione reached the San Carlo in a maelstrom of scraps of newspaper and hats torn from their owners' heads. As always, the Brigadier insisted on walking a step behind the Commissario, who strode along bareheaded, his eyes fixed on the ground. He was thinking about what he had learned from the priest regarding the operas' plots. *You like your fictional feelings masquerading onstage so much, Father? What's so great about people stabbing each other as they sing? I'd show you, if I could. Do you know how long the echo of a stabbing lasts? There's nothing pretty about a man screaming out his hatred every day for months, his guts spilling out endlessly from a gash in his belly.*

In the theater, the mood was very different from that of the previous evening. The lights were off, the clean-up completed.

The opulent entrance was chilly and silent. A young reporter, ensconced in an easy chair and bundled up in a heavy overcoat, sprang up like a jack-in-the-box.

"Good morning. Are you Commissario Ricciardi? I'm Luise from *Il Mattino*. May I ask you a few questions?"

"No. But you can go to the Questura, where Vice Questore Garzo will be happy to answer them."

"Actually my editor-in-chief, Signor Capece, told me that I had to speak with you, since you are directly conducting the investigation."

"Young man, please: don't make me waste time. I'm busy, so I will not answer any questions. Kindly be on your way."

Vezzi's dressing room, aside from the fact that the body had been removed, was the same as the previous evening. The blood had now caked and formed dark stains on the carpet, the sofa, the walls. In the corner, Ricciardi saw the image of the tenor who kept repeating his song, tears lining his face, his hand outstretched.

As he stood there, arms folded, his green gaze sombre, the strand of hair falling over his sharp nose, the Commissario wondered what the tenor could have wanted to ward off with that hand. And why he had then ended up seated, with his face in the mirror and a long glass shard in his artery. He walked over to the sofa, studied the coat. Assuming it had been placed there after the tenor's death, he thought, who had brought it back and why? A murderer who manages to flee the scene of the crime doesn't soon return, unless he's forced to. And with all those people around, who would be able to move freely about the dressing rooms? Sighing, Ricciardi called Maione over. It was time to take a closer look at the man singing in the corner, blood gushing from his throat.

Vezzi's secretary, Stefano Bassi, was a man who was visibly upset. He couldn't imagine his life without the Maestro.

"You have no idea, Commissario. You have no idea what

the Maestro meant to me. I can't believe all this is real. And in such an atrocious way!"

He spoke in a trembling voice, incoherently, wringing his hands. A neat, pleasant-looking man, with a dapper style and slender build, Bassi had always been the image of efficiency; but now, robbed of his point of reference, he didn't know where to turn. He adjusted his gold-rimmed glasses on his nose.

"There wasn't a moment when I left his side. But this damned habit of putting on his make-up and getting dressed by himself . . . It was a kind of superstition, an obsession, to ward off bad luck. Vezzi's vezzo, his fixation, he always said. I'll never hear him laugh again, or sing with that angelic voice. I can't believe it."

"Where were you yesterday, during the performance of *Cavalleria Rusticana*? When was the last time you saw him?"

"I was in the audience with the theater director; you can easily verify it. I didn't move the entire time. The troupe was quite good, by the way: especially the baritone, the one who played Alfio. We had left the Maestro earlier, when he went to his dressing room. He always said that no one should see him in costume offstage, that it was bad luck. He had a—how should I put it?—a strong-willed temperament, that's it. You could not contradict him. He was one of those people who go their own way, ploughing straight ahead, without deviating. He could be . . . demanding. But if you complied with him, by disappearing at the right moment, then he was the ideal boss."

"Disappearing? At the right moment? Meaning?"

"Meaning that he often asked to be left alone. To be free to do what he wanted. He was an artist, you know? A great artist; the greatest, in his field. *Il Duce* himself—"

"Considered him the greatest of all, a national pride, I know. And yesterday? Did you notice if he was in a bad mood, maybe, or different than usual?"

Bassi gave a nervous titter.

"Bad mood? I can see you didn't know him. The Maestro was always in a bad mood. He considered the whole world inferior to him and unworthy of coming between him and wherever he wanted to go. He swatted away anyone who got in his way with a wave of his hand, like you do with a fly. That's what he did last night, when he retreated to his dressing room an hour before the start of *Cavalleria*. He loved putting on his make-up alone, don't ask me why. Maybe it relaxed him. If you ask me, he didn't consider any make-up artist worthy of laying a hand on his face."

"A swell guy. Had you worked for him a long time?"

"For a year and a half. I think I'm the one who held out the longest. The guy before me ended up in the hospital with a broken nose. I fared better because, partly due to temperament, partly to necessity, I'm more tolerant. Then, too, the Maestro paid very well. How will I manage now?"

"As far as you know, did he have any enemies? Someone who might have had an interest in seeing him dead, I mean. Money, women. Whatever."

"You want to know if there was someone who had been wronged or whom the Maestro had mistreated in some way? Well, we could spend the whole day on it. But wanting to see him dead . . . you see, Commissario, the opera world is peculiar: many people live off the artists—impresarios, record producers, theater owners, people like me. When a great artist comes along, one that draws huge crowds of people, who sells out every time, then believe me, Commissario, nobody wants to see him dead, or even old or sick or demented. We all coddle him and gladly put up with tantrums, or a slap, from time to time."

"And outside of this world?"

Bassi again adjusted his glasses on his nose.

"Nothing in the Maestro's life was outside of the opera world. When one is that great and used to being viewed as such, he can't associate with anyone outside that circle. In a year and a half, I don't think I ever saw him speak to anyone who wasn't connected to the opera."

"How long had you been in the city?"

"This time? Three days. Enough time to prepare for the performance. The Maestro only attends the dress rehearsal and never in costume. He's the only one in regular clothes, the others wear their costumes. That's the way he liked it. We were coming from Rome, where we finalized arrangements for a tour in America that was to take place in the autumn. What we'll do now, I really don't know. I'll have to speak to Signor Marelli, the Maestro's manager and agent. He arrives this evening, by train."

'Yes, I know. I have to speak with him too. For now you may go. But don't leave the hotel, I might still need you.'

# XV

This Maestro Vezzi, Maione said when Bassi had gone, "must certainly have been a real bastard, *Commissa'*. He may have been talented, very talented, but he was a bastard. Yesterday, on the stage where we gathered everyone together, I heard them say that he showed up at the dress rehearsal two hours late. And since he had told them he wanted to rehearse his opera first, everyone had to wait for him. Then when the orchestra conductor had the nerve to complain, he yelled insults at him for ten minutes. He humiliated him badly. Do you want to speak with the conductor?"

Ricciardi nodded, distracted. Both Bassi and don Pierino had said something that tickled his intuition, but he couldn't quite put his finger on it. What was it? It would come back to him.

The orchestra conductor, Maestro Mariano Pelosi, was a drinker. Ricciardi noticed it right away, as soon as he looked at him, even before the man sat down in front of the desk in the stage manager's small office.

He could tell by the network of little veins on the man's nose, the vacuous, watery eyes, the slight hesitation in his speech and the faint tremor in his hands. He had seen many like him in his perennial search for the causes of sorrow. Wine was a solace for weakness as well as a stimulus to extreme actions. In wine it was easy to find the courage to commit a crime, toppling the barriers of conscience and venting one's frustrations.

"We are all shocked, Commissario. The theater is a place of joy and feeling. At the theater, people expect to find—and *should* find—respite from the madness of everyday life. And in these times there is plenty of madness, don't you think? But you don't expect that madness to turn up just steps from the stage. It's just like *Pagliacci*, when Canio kills Nedda and Silvio onstage, and the audience doesn't immediately know if it's reality or make-believe. You never know at first, whether it's reality or fiction."

"Your relationship with Vezzi, Maestro. They tell me that during the dress rehearsal you two quarrelled, so to speak."

"With Vezzi, God had some fun, Commissario. It amused Him to bestow an immense talent on a worthless man. Truly worthless. Onstage he was fantastic, in my forty-year career I had never come across such a voice, such a presence. And believe me, I've heard many. Caruso himself, the great Caruso, doesn't have the range, the conviction of Vezzi's voice. Not to mention the ability to command the stage, to perform. It never even seemed like he was acting. The difference between him and the other singers was sometimes so strident that it caused the orchestra to slip up. You see, his bravura stripped others of their conviction, left them hesitant. Fellow singers, orchestra members, the stage manager himself. Even me."

"And so? The evening of the rehearsal?"

"The evening of the rehearsal, yes. We had been ready for almost two hours. We could and should have rehearsed *Cavalleria Rusticana*, because that's the right order, but Vezzi had demanded that we begin with his opera, because he didn't want to wait around. The dress rehearsal—I don't know if you're aware of this, Commissario—is in every way identical to a performance, with people in their stage costumes. Vezzi didn't want to wear his costume prior to going onstage before the public. It is, or rather *was*, an obsession with him. This alone confuses those who have to perform with him, making him seem like an interloper. On that same occasion, he violently found fault with both Bartino, the baritone who plays Tonio, and Siloty, the Hungarian soprano who plays Nedda. Plus, his lateness . . . I have certain medications I must take at a specific time. Instead, there I was trapped in the pit with my musicians. I was very, very anxious. So, when he arrived without apologizing or anything, as calmly as though he were right on time, I saw red. But even then, I did not lose my self-control: he could have been my son, given our ages. But he . . . he . . . began yelling. That I was an old lunatic, a failure . . . "

As he spoke, Pelosi began to seem visibly upset. His lips trembled and his jaw muscle quivered in an attempt to hold back tears. A useless attempt, since big drops rolled down his stubbly cheeks. Maione, embarrassed, gave a little cough. Ricciardi, on the other hand, stared at the conductor impassively, as if he hadn't noticed his display of emotion.

"And you? How did you feel, being attacked in front of everyone, and being in the right besides?"

"In the lives of everyone, Commissario, there are decision points. The road forks, there's a right way and a wrong way. The trouble is that at that moment you don't know which is which. You always think you can go back, whenever you want. Instead, you can't go back, ever. I took my wrong road many years ago, too many not to realize it every day. I know it, others know it. But music is my life, the only thing I know how to do. So I try to do it the best I can, and not involve others in my mistakes. Vezzi was a luminary and we all have . . . had something to gain from his presence. His insults hurt me, it's true: I think he was a genius as well as a profoundly egotistical and malicious man, as geniuses often are. But, as you must already have verified, I did not move from the orchestra pit the entire evening. I am not your killer."

When Pelosi left, Maione said, "The more I hear people talk, the more convinced I am that this Vezzi was a bastard. I wonder, *Commissa'*, how it must be to work for someone whom you loathe. Take you, for instance: to be truthful, it's not like you're very outgoing. But we know what you're thinking. Almost all of us, at least. In any case, it's out of the question that those who were onstage, the orchestra included, could have killed him."

Ricciardi seemed to be following his own line of thinking. "Recapping what we have," he said, "Vezzi dies with his throat cut, or at least with a glass shard in his carotid artery. We find him sitting in the dressing room, his face on the dressing tabletop. Blood everywhere, except on the coat, the scarf, the hat and also one of the sofa cushions. The window open, the door locked. And we know that, for a singer, the first concern is a draught, especially before going onstage. No one who isn't known is allowed to enter the dressing rooms. Everyone connected to Vezzi for better or for worse was in the concert hall, under the eyes of everyone else, and no one budged. Everyone hated him, but no one had anything to gain from harming him. A fine conundrum."

"The detail about the coat, scarf and hat seems significant to me," Maione said. "So, you think someone entered, covered up, and then escaped through the window, after killing Vezzi?"

"No. The clothes would be stained. Plus, there's a little armoire in the dressing room, with a hatbox. Vezzi was an orderly man, you can tell by the way he kept his things, the fact that he put his make-up on himself, the toiletries in the bathroom. Someone took those items out and then left them on the floor and on the sofa. But why? And how come the whole sofa is covered in blood, except for a small cushion? No, it doesn't add up. Something is still missing and we have to find it."

Ricciardi did not mention a further element: the tears on the clown's cheek as he sang, the words he spoke, the outstretched hand.

"Do one thing, Maione: go to the hotel where Vezzi had been

staying. Ask his secretary, that Bassi, which one it is. Ask if anyone remembers what he was wearing when he left there yesterday, if there was anything unusual; if he went somewhere else first. Also what time he left on the evening of the dress rehearsal. I want to know why he was late. I'll stay here a little longer."

Outside the stage manager's office, along with Lasio himself, was the theater director, Spinelli. Aside from the little Duke's agitation as he bounced up and down, the same as the night before, there was a new deference, a more subdued attitude. Evidently he had become aware of the ineffectiveness of his reports when it came to having the rude, disrespectful Commissario taken off the investigation. His tone was still pompous, however.

"Good day, Commissario. I didn't want to disturb you while you were busy with your interrogations. I wanted to say that I am at your complete disposal, as is the theater's entire staff. We have been informed of the importance assigned to finding the vile killer, and it is our intention to provide you with our full cooperation."

Ricciardi stared at Spinelli coldly. Stiff and offended, the man seemed to be trying to put a good face on it as he followed higher instructions from above.

"I don't doubt it, Duke. I don't doubt it. In that case, I would like a complete schedule of the performances presented recently, let's say from when the staging of the operas began up until today. I also want to know the dates when Vezzi was present at the theater." He turned to the stage manager. "Tell me, from which entrance is it quicker to get to the dressing rooms?"

Lasio ran a hand through his red hair; he was one of those people who seem rumpled even though they're not, maybe because of his pale, freckled complexion or his rebellious head of hair. He wore a shirt that sported a stiff collar with rounded tabs and he had loosened his tie. He wasn't wearing a jacket and his vest was unbuttoned.

"Definitely the side door, which leads to the street near the gate to the gardens. From there it's just one flight of stairs and you're near the dressing rooms. The staircase is narrow and half-hidden and you have to know it's there, but it's the most direct route. The stage performers use it, if they need to leave the theater momentarily during the performance."

"And is there someone at the door?"

"Not during the performance. We turn off the lights in the vestibule, to concentrate staff at the main entrance, and lock the door. But there's a smaller door beside it."

Ricciardi pondered this.

"Which staff, aside from the stage performers, has access to the dressing rooms during the performance?"

"Under normal circumstances, no one. Except for possible medical personnel, naturally, and wardrobe staff, to bring down costumes requiring last-minute adjustments. But I insist that this coming and going be kept to a minimum. The more noise, distractions, confusion there is, the greater the chance of slipping up on the entrance cues. There's nothing worse than a delayed or early entrance, believe me."

"I see. And where is the wardrobe room?"

The theater director spoke up.

"On the fourth floor, Commissario. There's a utility lift, used for bringing the costume changes quickly to the dressing rooms. In certain operas there are dozens of costumes that have to be changed, between acts. I recall an occasion on which . . . "

"Yes, I imagine," Ricciardi cut him short, "but now I'd like to see the wardrobe staff. Are they working?"

"Certainly. They're always working." The theater director looked miffed again, as if he had been slapped in the face, but he was more prudent than the previous evening. He added: "Nevertheless it will be a pleasure, for the staff, to be able to cooperate."

# XVI

Wardrobe, on the fourth floor, could be reached via a narrow staircase or the utility lift. Ricciardi decided to inspect both routes, going up in the chugging cage, supported by creaking cables, and coming down the steep steps. From the landing there was a spectacular bird's-eye view of both the stage and the orchestra pit. The view of the concert hall itself was obstructed by a heavy curtain. At the end of a long corridor was a door leading to a whole other world.

It looked like a dream factory. Silks and brocades, fabrics woven in gold and silver. Every colour imaginable, from red to purple, from yellow to blue to green. Headdresses from various eras, lined up one beside the other on large hat racks. Stovepipe hats, Roman and Viking helmets, complicated Egyptian hairpieces. Tulle, veils, delicate ballet slippers and heavy military boots. Among all these fabrics were numerous women all dressed the same, like Signora Lilla: blue smock with heavy scissors hanging from a ribbon around the neck, hair tied back and partially covered with a white cap. They moved skilfully through the seeming disorder, cutting, sewing and ironing. Outside, the wind howled, while the sun's intermittent rays, broken by clouds that chased one another across the sky, filtered down from the high windows.

Ricciardi, with his grey overcoat and dark colouring, was the only bleak spot in that riot of colour. His steady gaze surveyed the large room from top to bottom as the theater director bounced up and down at his side.

Signora Lilla came towards them brusquely, looking annoyed. This was her realm and she did not tolerate interference. Her belligerent stance made her look even more mastodontic.

"Good morning. What can I do for you? We're behind on our work, we have to adjust all of poor Vezzi's costumes for his replacement."

The theater director stepped forwards.

"Good morning. Madam, I must ask you to please place yourself, along with your co-workers, at the complete disposal of the Commissario, who requires you in order to complete his investigation. This should be your foremost duty."

Signora Lilla shrugged.

"Just as long as you keep it in mind, when the costumes for tonight's performance aren't ready. What would you like to know?"

Ricciardi spoke to her, not bothering with a greeting, and keeping his hands in the pockets of his overcoat.

"How do you assign the work? Is there someone who looks after specific singers, for example?"

"No. Everyone has her own specialty: some sew, some prefer to cut. They can all do everything—the wardrobe department is the pride of this theater—but each of them can do something better than the others and I use her that way."

"So then, Vezzi did not have a seamstress who saw to him in particular?"

"God forbid! Vezzi drove the girls crazy. If one of them had had to look after him all by herself, then I'd tell you who killed him. No, no: Maria and Addolorata did the fitting the other day. The clown costume, I mean. Canio's costumes were already done, from the last time. The work was then completed by Lucia, who is the best at adding the finishing touches, and Maddalena whom you met. She had come down with me to deliver the costume. She made the final adjustment. She's young but she's getting to be quite good."

"Where are these four? Can I see them?"

"Yes, but hopefully you won't take up too much of our time. They're back there."

Ricciardi walked over to a large table where the four young women were sitting. The clown costume was on the tabletop and they were all working on it, eyes lowered. Seen like that, in uniform and with scissors and needles in hand, they all looked alike. The Commissario was barely able to recognize the pale girl whom he had seen the evening before, nearly staggering under the weight of the costume.

"Good day, everyone. How is the work going?"

A murmur of assent, but it was Signora Lilla who responded.

"It's quite a job. Vezzi was a tall, heavyset man, with a belly. His replacement is short and thin: I don't know where that voice of his comes from. We have to cut the costumes from scratch."

Ricciardi spoke to the girls again.

"Does anyone remember having seen or heard anything unusual in Vezzi's dressing room? A word, an object. A change in mood."

One of the four, a brunette with lively eyes, looked up at the Commissario and gave a half-smile.

"Vezzi's mood never changed, Commissario: it was always black, like this button. At best, he might give you a pat on the ass. At worst, it was as if you were invisible."

"Maria! Be careful what you say!" Signora Lilla said. But you could tell she was amused. Ricciardi saw that they weren't getting anywhere.

"If you should think of anything else, let me know: either come to the Questura, or tell Signora Lilla."

Meanwhile, the stage manager had entered; his arrival triggered a dramatic change in Signora Lilla, who, blushing, lowered her eyes and nervously smoothed her wiry blonde hair with both hands.

Lasio spoke to Ricciardi: "Commissario, there's a man asking for you at the front entrance, he says he's Dr. Modo, the medical examiner. Good morning, Signora Lilla."

The woman replied in a soft, velvety voice, very different to the sharp, brusque tone she'd been using until then.

"Good morning to you, my dear Signor Lasio. Gentlemen, we are at your disposal: come back whenever you like."

# XVII

Dr. Modo stood waiting at the main entrance, smoking and huddled inside the vestibule to avoid the cold wind. As soon as he saw Ricciardi, he smiled.

"Spending the morning at the theater, huh? Addicted to it."

The Commissario made a face.

"Hello, Doctor. What are you doing here? Couldn't stand being away from me any longer, right?"

"How about it, will you buy me lunch?"

"Out of the question. I was thinking of just a pizza, from the usual cart. Come on, a *sfogliatella* and coffee at Gambrinus: seems like a fair compromise to me."

"Spendthrift. And yet they say you're loaded. Fine, I'll settle for that: anything to get out of the cold."

Walking against the wind, they covered the short distance to the cafè in silence, the doctor holding on to his hat and tightening his coat collar, Ricciardi with his hands in his pockets and his hair blowing about. He was thinking about the evidence gathered that morning. He felt like he was holding the pieces of a wooden puppet which he couldn't seem to put together. He also had the nagging sensation that he had not given proper importance to something. But to what?

The two men went in, rubbing their hands, and sat down at Ricciardi's usual table, the one near the window that looked out on to Via Chiaia. The doctor puffed, taking off his hat, coat and gloves.

"When was the last time we saw such weather in late March?

You're a country boy from the mountains, but I'm from the coast and I'm telling you that as a kid I would already be diving off the rocks at Marechiaro by this time. Even in the Alps, during the war, it wasn't this cold in March."

"Don't complain; you'll keep better this way. Like your cadavers."

"Hold on, wait a second: maybe I'm hearing voices, like Joan of Arc. I thought I heard a wisecrack: but aren't you Commissario Ricciardi? The gloomy Commissario Ricciardi, the man who never smiles?"

"And in fact I'm not smiling. So, what can you tell me? You beat me to it—I would have come by your place this afternoon."

Modo nodded dejectedly.

"Listen, I've never felt so much pressure to work quickly: even from Rome, from the Ministry. Who on earth did they kill, the Pope? Your pal Garzo, always so *simpatico*, sent that clerk of his, Ponte, to see me twice this morning. If there were any results from the lab tests and the autopsy, the Questura wanted to know immediately."

"And are there any results?"

"Well, I don't know. I'm not sure. I'd say that the considerations I shared with you last night remain valid. However there is something strange; more a feeling than anything else. Still, it's a feeling."

The waiter appeared. Ricciardi ordered two coffees and two *sfogliatelle*.

"What do you mean, a feeling? Are there feelings, in your profession? Isn't it all just scientific rigour?"

"Ah, there we go, now I recognize you: the sarcastic Commissario Ricciardi, ready to relegate science to second place. But science can help your feelings. It can confirm them, and it can prove them wrong."

The waiter returned, bringing their order. The doctor bit

into his *sfogliatella*, famished. His greying moustache turned white from the powdered sugar dusting the flaky pastry; each mouthful was accompanied by moans of pleasure.

"Mmm . . . ask me what I love about this city, and I'll tell you: the *sfogliatelle*! Not the sea, not the sun; the *sfogliatelle*."

Ricciardi, who, on alternating days, lived on *sfogliatella* and pizza, tried to draw the doctor's attention back to Vezzi.

"Do you mind telling me about this feeling of yours? I realize you're getting old, but lately you've been having trouble maintaining your concentration."

"Listen, I'm more alert at fifty-five than two consulting doctors of twenty-seven, and you know it. So then: remember I told you, there at the scene, about the ecchymosis under the left eye? We talked about a punch, a blow."

Ricciardi nodded.

"He was struck, hard. His cheekbone was actually fractured, not a big deal, but still, fractured."

"So?"

"So it's not possible that a haematoma would be so circumscribed. Do you have any idea how little time it takes for a haematoma to form? From a blow of that kind? He should have had a balloon under his eye. Instead, there was just a little bruise."

"Which means?"

"Which means—and I know you already know because I can see it in your eyes—that our great tenor, friend of the Ministers of the Fasces, damn him, was already dead when he was struck or had just a few seconds of breath left. His black heart wasn't pumping out much anymore."

"You know, Bruno, one of these days you're going to get beaten up over those anti-fascist comments, I'm telling you."

Modo grinned broadly, his mouth full of pastry cream and coffee, which he had been wolfing down as he talked.

"But I have friends in the police!"

"Yeah, sure. So, he was already dead or dying. Then why would they have had to hit him, if he was already dead?"

Ricciardi kept his eyes fixed on the doctor, who had his back to the window. Behind him, the little girl without a left arm, the marks of the tram wheels on her small battered chest, held out the bundle of rags to them: "This is my daughter. I feed her and bathe her." The Commissario sighed.

"Is something wrong?" Modo asked, noticing Ricciardi's expression grow pained all of a sudden.

"A hint of a migraine. Just a slight headache."

And a sea of despair, that attachment to life that no longer wants you, that moment when the hands cling to a prop before plunging into the void. "*This is my daughter. I feed her and bathe her.*" Dying under a tram, maybe to retrieve a stuffed rag doll that somehow ended up in the street. The sorrow. All that sorrow.

"You're an odd duck, Ricciardi. The oddest there is, everyone says so. You know, people are afraid of your silences, your determination. It's as if you want vengeance. But for what?"

"Look, Doctor, I enjoy talking with you. You're capable and decent. If you have something more to give, you give it, and that's no small matter in these times. But don't ask anything more of me, please, if you want me to continue talking to you."

"Whatever you say. I apologize. It's just that, working together, one can't help caring . . . you have a sorrowful expression at times. And I know sorrow, believe me."

No, you don't know it, Ricciardi thought. You know wounds and expressions of grief. But not sorrow. That comes afterwards, and poisons the air you breathe. It leaves a kind of sickly-sweet stench that lingers in your nose. The putrefaction of the soul.

"Thank you, Doctor. Without you, I would have already killed myself. I'll let you know if there are any developments in the investigation. One thing I'm curious about," Ricciardi added as he stood up, "why did you tell me about the bruise and not Ponte, the clerk?"

"Because your pal Garzo wears a black suit, that's why, whereas you . . . only your disposition is black. Pay the bill on your way out: a deal is a deal."

Ricciardi found both Maione and Ponte waiting outside his office. He nodded at the Brigadier, ignoring the clerk. He entered the room followed by Maione, who took off his overcoat and was about to close the door when the clerk stuck his head in.

"Excuse me, sir, but I don't want to get in any trouble. Vice Questore Garzo said that you were to see him the very minute you came in. He didn't even go out to lunch!"

"If it's so urgent that he talk with the Commissario, why doesn't he come here himself?" Maione asked sarcastically.

"Are you crazy, *Brigadie'*? That one only leaves the office to go and see the signor Questore! Please, sir, I beg you, don't make me get me in trouble."

"I'm busy right now, Ponte, I'm conducting an investigation, as the Vice Questore knows—or should know. If he has any information that can help me, have him send it to me. If not, let him put it in writing that I should go and see him instead of doing my job. He himself told me to set everything else aside."

Ponte gave a long sigh. "All right, sir, I understand. I'll tell him what you said, may God help me. As you wish."

When the clerk left, Maione sat down and pulled out a notebook.

"So then. Vezzi stayed at the Vesuvio, on the waterfront, the same hotel he always stays at whenever he comes to Naples. They arrived the evening of the twenty-first, by train, he and Bassi, the secretary. The hotel staff hated him—so what else is new. They say he chewed out anyone who came within sight, nothing ever satisfied him, and so on. However, nothing unusual happened, there were no quarrels that would suggest that anyone might do something. The dress rehearsal was scheduled for six o'clock on Monday, the twenty-third. Vezzi left the hotel at four and went straight back late in the evening, after the rehearsal. The doorman remembers him well, because he asked him if he needed a carriage and he told him to mind his own business. Yesterday, instead, he left at six to go to the theater, and was wearing a long black coat, the one we've seen, a broad-brimmed hat, also black, and a white wool scarf which he used to shield his face from the wind. When the doorman wished him good luck, Vezzi made *corna* at him and gave him a dirty look. That's everything. Oh, by the way: the hotel is right on the sea."

Ricciardi had listened closely, his hands clasped in front of his mouth and his eyes never leaving Maione.

"What time are they due to arrive, the manager and Vezzi's wife?"

"Two hours from now, at Mergellina station," Maione said, checking his wristwatch.

"All right then, send Bassi in. There's something I need to understand."

## XVIII

Vezzi's secretary appeared, dapper and elegant as always; hair neatly parted in the centre, freshly shaved, gold-rimmed glasses that he nervously kept adjusting on his nose.

"Should I be worried, Commissario? I'm not a suspect, am I? I'll remind you that I spent the evening sitting next to the theater director, in the front row."

Ricciardi made a slight wave of annoyance, as if to chase away an insect.

"No, Bassi. I wouldn't say so. But there is one thing I'd like to know. You said that, to please Vezzi, an assistant had to 'be able to disappear at the right moment, leaving him free.' Explain it to me more clearly. What does that mean, exactly?"

Bassi seemed caught off guard. He adjusted his glasses on his nose with his right index finger.

"Exactly? Well, in practical terms it means that the Maestro insisted on . . . well, discretion. You had to understand him even before he spoke, like all individuals endowed with a big ego."

"Look, Bassi, I asked you a specific question. Believe me, we're not in a convent here; there's nothing we haven't heard in this place. I know you meant something by it and I demand that you tell me what it was."

Bassi instantly lost his self-confidence. He went on speaking in a submissive tone.

"The Maestro had his weaknesses. Who doesn't? He was a

man who sought gratification, anywhere, no matter what the circumstances. And he liked women: especially those of other men. I often thought that he couldn't stand the idea that a woman might prefer someone else. Anyone else. So he took her. Or tried to take her. Though normally he managed to."

"But wasn't he married? Isn't it his wife who is arriving by train?"

"Well, married so to speak. His wife is, in a word, the kind of woman . . . she was a singer, you know. A contralto. She gave it up when they married, ten years ago. Then, after the death of their child—from diphtheria, five years ago—they virtually stopped speaking to one another. They each led their own lives. But you see, Commissario, the Maestro was a personal friend of *Il Duce*. The family cannot be destroyed. So formally they stayed together. But only formally."

"I see. So Vezzi busied himself elsewhere. And here, in Naples? How was he, these past days? Did he do anything, did he go anywhere?"

"I don't know, Commissario. When he . . . was busy, the Maestro simply dismissed me. He'd say: 'I have no further need of you; I'll see you at seven, or eight, or nine,' whatever. I understood, and I kept away. Still, there was always something to do, so . . . "

"And in the past few days did he dismiss you?"

"Yes, on Monday, the day of the dress rehearsal."

"And did he say anything to you?"

"Yes, something odd: he asked me where you caught tram number seven from."

As soon as Bassi left, Ricciardi asked Maione what route tram number seven followed. The Brigadier went off for a few minutes, and when he returned, he was the usual font of information.

"So then, *Commissa'*: there are two number seven trams. The red seven, that leaves from Piazza Plebiscito and goes to

Piazza Vanvitelli, on the hill above the Vomero; and the black seven, that starts at Piazza Dante and also goes to the Vomero, but to Piazzale di San Martino. Antonelli told me and he knows all the transportation routes in the city, proving that those guys in the records department don't do a thing from morning till night. Now, the black seven is called the 'poor lovers' tram,' because it leads to a little wood with panoramic views of the city, where he says couples who can't afford a room get together. The red seven, on the other hand, is used by those who work in the centre and live in the new houses. Which one would Vezzi have taken?"

"The black seven. For certain."

So Ricciardi decided to fill the time remaining before the arrival of Vezzi's wife and his manager by making a quick on-site inspection of the black seven line. In actuality, he admitted to himself, it was also an excuse to avoid giving Garzo a report that by now was overdue. He didn't like the idea of presenting sketchy or incomplete theories, but neither could he concoct a story out of whole cloth and pretend he was on the trail of a murderer he had already identified. So he told Maione to stay there and hold down the fort, in case someone came to make a spontaneous statement, and set off on foot towards Piazza Dante.

The wind had lessened a little, and clouds were thickening: maybe it would rain. Early in the afternoon the street was crowded with pedestrians and street vendors. For sixty years now its name had been Via Roma, but for Neapolitans it was and would remain Via Toledo, like when it was built under the Spaniards. And it would remain the boundary, the throbbing border line between the two souls of the city, which was alternately invaded and possessed by one or the other. The shouts and calls of vendors split the air, urchins ran barefoot, chasing one another. Beggars sat huddled beside the walls of buildings, near the entrance to churches. On the left side, the maze of numerous back alleys intersecting the street revealed the desolate, volatile scene of the old Quartieri Spagnoli.

As he walked along, Ricciardi continued to reflect: why the tram? A carriage, or one of the city's fifty taxis, would have been a more logical choice. Or even the funicular, the beautiful, modern Funicolare Centrale that had been open for three years; the real reason why the new quarter was becoming increasingly populated, attracting the attention of the middle class more and more. But otherwise, the Vomero was still farmland, with flocks of sheep and goats and farmsteads. And a few beautiful aristocratic villas, for vacationing in the clean air.

The only reason why Vezzi would have preferred the tram was anonymity. So he wouldn't be recognized. Why? Because the tenor's intention wasn't simply to take a nice vigorous walk. Rather a different kind of walk. Ergo a courtesy visit to some aristocratic friend could also be ruled out.

The tram station in Piazza Dante was right at the base of the long incline that led to the Vomero. Ricciardi bought a ticket and sat down near a window. On the street, toward Port'Alba, he saw the vision of a Camorrist mobster who had been stabbed during a settling of accounts. His killer had quickly been arrested: a young man who had aspired to make his way up in society and instead would rot in prison for thirty years. The image of the dead man, big and tall, his hands on his hips, was laughing his head off. Literally, because his neck was slashed from ear to ear; you could see the blood gurgling through the wound and bubbles of air from his last breath. He was mocking his murderer and his lack of courage: a fatal miscalculation. With a jolt, the tram started off.

As it climbed, the houses gradually thinned out, though Ricciardi observed numerous building sites. A city under construction, which a little at a time was taking over the countryside. The previous year's earthquake had led to needed reinforcing and restoration; there had been some collapses and some deaths, though it was Irpinia, some distance away, that had been devastated. But there were also new buildings, new streets and roads. Other districts to keep an eye on, additional wealth and new crimes and offences, the Commissario thought with a sigh.

The cold wind gradually grew stronger as the tram clambered up the hill, trudging along; Ricciardi could tell from the swaying of the vegetation, that was now more dense. Trees, shrubs, cultivated fields, dirt paths leading into the countryside; here and there a villa surrounded by palm trees. On either side of the road—the tramway running down the middle of it—were occasional shacks with women washing clothes and children playing outdoors. A boy with a dog and two goats tied to a rope was selling ricotta cheese and bread to a small group of bricklayers at a construction site. One of them, standing a little apart, had his head bent in an unnatural way. The Commissario looked away: one of the thousands of workplace accidents, which no one ever heard about.

The tram reached the end of the line, in the new square in front of the military prison. Ricciardi approached the man in the ticket office and asked if there was a boarding house or hotel in the immediate vicinity. When he got directions, he set out towards a small, low building not far away, where a green metal plate bore a yellow inscription: Pensione Belvedere.

The landlady was initially suspicious. Then, when he showed his ID, she admitted that she recalled the portly gentleman who "spoke like a foreigner, a northerner," who had come on Monday, the twenty-third. He had remained in his room for three hours, and had been joined by the signora. The signora had arrived on her own, they had not come together. Yes, she had said "his room": the gentleman had rented it for three months, paying in advance. Did the Commissario wish to see it?

Ricciardi found himself in a clean room, with a magnificent

view from the window. No personal items, except a shaving brush, soap and a razor near a sink in the corner. No trace of any female presence, nothing in the chest of drawers, nothing in the armoire other than a new dressing gown, apparently never worn. He fingered it, as if wanting to feel its texture. On the shoulder, a long blonde hair.

As he was leaving, the Commissario told the landlady that she could consider the room vacant, since the tenant was not coming back. The woman did not hide her disappointment.

"I was hoping he would renew. Even though he didn't answer me when I asked him. He left in a hurry."

"What do you mean, renew? Didn't he pay for three months, starting Monday the twenty-third?"

"No, *Commissa'*. Three months, beginning last December twentieth. That was when they came for the first time. Work was still underway on the new piazzale."

"And the woman who joined him? Was it always the same one?"

"Yes, Commissario. Always the same one. You could tell she was young; she came on her own, separately."

"Can you describe her?"

"No, truthfully, no. She wore a hat, a scarf, a heavy coat; I never saw her face. She didn't even respond when I greeted her, I never heard her voice. Too bad, though; he seemed happy. And what nice tips he left me!"

The news shed new light on events, Ricciardi thought as he walked down the slope leading to the panoramic piazzale and the belvedere. Vezzi had come to Naples in December, then: so that was the other time Bassi had hinted at. That was the detail that had been tickling his intuition, that he had not been able to put his finger on immediately. But there was something else in what don Pierino had said, that still wouldn't come to him. What was it?

The tram wouldn't leave for another fifteen minutes. He

decided to check out the view from the new belvedere. The city stretched out below him, under a sky increasingly heavy with rain. Seeing it like that, as the first lights began to appear, it did not look like it was seething with passions or emotions. But Ricciardi knew how many layers there were, beneath that apparent tranquillity. No crime, only safety and well-being dictated by the regime. So it was ordained, by decree. Yet the dead kept vigil in the streets, in homes, demanding peace and justice.

He went up to the low wall: beneath him, the winding steps of Via Pedamentina which from San Martino led to Corso Vittorio Emanuele. A long, charming street, which flanked a slope of dense vegetation. The hanging lamps that illuminated the steps swayed in the wind. But the late afternoon rays still lit up a small park with benches, a trysting spot for lovers who could not afford a room for three hours much less for three months.

Ricciardi saw two couples on the benches. A sailor was trying to embrace a girl who laughingly pushed him away. And a slim, elegant young man, perhaps a student, was holding the hand of a woman who stared at him dreamily. Ricciardi looked away. A short distance from the sailor he saw a man sitting on the ground holding both arms tightly around his stomach as if hugging himself. A yellowish foam bubbling with air oozed from his mouth. His eyes were glassy. Even from a distance like that, the Commissario could make out his words: "*I can't live without you. I can't live without you. I can't live without you . . .* " He poisoned himself, Ricciardi thought. Barbiturates, acid, bleach. Does anything ever change?

A little further back the body of a young woman swung from a branch, hanging from a piece of cloth, a scarf maybe. She looked like a belated winter fruit, like a bunch of grapes that had escaped the harvest and had not yet dried up. Eyes bulging, her face purple, her tongue horribly swollen and bluish, hanging from her bloated lips. Her neck stretched by gravity's pull, legs and arms limp and composed. She kept repeating: "*Why, my love? Why, my love*?" A place for lovers, Ricciardi thought. He had seen others "haunted" like that: people went to seek peace where they had been happy, not knowing that there was no peace, even in death.

As he observed the living and the dead, he recalled the advertisement for a wonder drug, which he often saw in the newspaper. Before and after treatment.

Before and after love.

The tram sounded its horn. His expression unchanged, Ricciardi turned and began slowly walking up the slope.

# XIX

The church of Santa Maria degli Angeli was freezing. The wind whistled relentlessly down the nave and inside the dome, where light filtered in from a sun that shed no warmth. In the pews in front of the altar several old women intoned an endless chant in the mangled words of a forgotten language, imploring God's mercy and that of the saints.

In the back, a woman was hiding in the shadows. Her head was bowed, and her blonde hair and her face were concealed by a large black shawl. She was hiding her beauty, her body, her blue eyes. She would have liked to pray, but she didn't have the heart.

She looked up at the fresco on the dome, stained with dampness, depicting paradise.

The woman smiled sadly. A ruined paradise, wrecked to pieces. A longed-for paradise, painted in vivid colours and then lost. It seemed like the story of her life. She had imagined a new life, a new love. She looked around and saw the beautiful illustrations of the life of Mary. The purity, the innocence. Whereas she . . . she had not entered to seek forgiveness: she wasn't sorry about the betrayal. She had gone there to think about how she could have fallen into hell after being so close to paradise.

Exactly twenty-four hours after Vezzi's murder, Ricciardi returned to the Questura. As expected, he found both Maione and Ponte outside his office. The air was electric, there had obviously been more than a few words between the two. The Brigadier's eyes were bloodshot, the clerk's lips were quivering.

"Finally, sir! I don't know what to tell the Vice Questore anymore. The Brigadier here is taking it out on me. I'll cover for you as much as I can, but . . . "

"What do you think you're covering, you ass-licker's lackey? You have to let us do our job, can't you get it into your head? How are we supposed to get anywhere if we have to report every five minutes?"

Ricciardi thought it appropriate to intervene.

"Never mind, Maione. I'll take care of it. You go and pick up the manager and the wife, who are about to arrive. Ponte, come with me to Garzo."

This time the Vice Questore did not get up to welcome Ricciardi. Nor did he tell him to sit down.

"So then, Ricciardi. I'm only going to ask this once. Where are you with it?"

You. Not we.

"I'm investigating. If there were any new developments I would have reported to you, of course. Isn't that what we agreed?"

"You're not the one asking the questions!" Garzo snapped. "Do you have any idea of the pressure we're under? We get phonograms from Rome every hour. It's all the newspapers are talking about. Il Mattino called to vigorously protest the way you treated a reporter, a certain Luise, this morning at the theater. Those guys will retaliate, Ricciardi: you know that, don't you? It doesn't take much to go from 'brilliant investigator' to a 'bumbler' groping in the dark. What am I supposed to tell the Questore? And what is he supposed to tell Rome? Vezzi's death has sparked more contact between *Il Duce*'s office and the city's High Commissioner than last year's earthquake. You must, I say must, give me something."

"I don't speak without having something to say, Vice Questore. Never. If I give you a fact it means I have one."

Garzo's confidence was crumbling.

"But I don't know what to tell them! Please, put yourself in my shoes. I can't let them see that I don't know anything!"

"Tell them it's probably a crime of passion. Isn't there always passion behind a crime? Tell them that. Whatever the solution turns out to be, you'll have been correct."

Garzo lit up.

"You're right, Ricciardi. *Bravo, bravissimo*! This will satisfy them, for a while. But I urge you: don't keep me in the dark. If you should uncover anything else, please, tell me immediately."

"Of course, you have my word. But keep the press and Ponte out of my way."

"Consider it done. Keep up the good work, Ricciardi."

Returning to his office, Ricciardi tried to organize his thoughts. Vezzi had come to Naples with Bassi, in an official capacity, just before Christmas; he had stayed a few days, had rented the room at the Pensione Belvedere. He had been there on the day of the dress rehearsal as well, that was the reason he was late. The long blonde hair on the dressing gown. Ergo, a woman: and a woman to keep carefully hidden.

There seemed to be several people with good reasons to want to see him dead, or at least take their revenge: the orchestra conductor, for example. Or Bassi himself, continually humiliated. Or any of the baritones, sopranos and valets.

But Ricciardi had the idea that the people in the theater would be unlikely to give vent to their egos that way: opportunity, first of all. And then being used to acting, to fiction. No, he couldn't see a singer or an orchestra player plan and implement such a fierce crime out of resentment. Besides, all aspects of the murder pointed to impulse: the scuffle, the broken mirror, all that blood. Whatever had happened, it was certainly not a premeditated crime. And the tenor was alone in his dressing room before being killed, putting on his make-up and getting ready to perform. Vezzi's vezzo, his fixed routine. So who could it have been? Ricciardi knew that he had to look for the two old culprits: hunger and love. One or both of them. Hunger and love: at the root of any killing.

Maione popped his head in the door.

"*Commissa'*, the manager and the signora are in the waiting room. Who do you want to see first?"

Mario Marelli was a businessman; you could tell from his clothing, the way he spoke, his gestures. Even his facial features: a square, strong-willed jaw, a prominent nose and clear blue eyes under bushy eyebrows. His well-trimmed hair, sleeked back with pomade, was barely greying at the temples; a dark tie, perfectly knotted, graced an impeccable white shirt with a rounded collar. The buttons of his waistcoat appeared beneath a double-breasted, brown pinstriped jacket, and a gold watch chain hung out of the vest pocket.

"Commissario, I won't waste your time and mine by pretending to be grieving. Vezzi was a dreadful individual, as you have probably gathered; and if you haven't, I will tell you so. I never met a single person who liked him, in the ten years that I rendered my services on his behalf. Aside from the powers that be in Rome, of course. When it came to licking the feet of those in power, he was *bravissimo*."

"How come you weren't with him, in Naples?"

"I had been here for the preliminary arrangements, before Christmas: that's when the terms of the contract, payments and all the other terms and conditions are settled. Later, at the time of the performance, it's not necessary for the manager to be present. In this case, the less time I spent with that degenerate, the better off I was. So I made damn sure I didn't go with him."

"As far as you remember, when you came before Christmas did Vezzi go off on his own for a period of time?"

"Vezzi? For the entire time. Maybe I didn't make myself clear: he left it to me to deal with the contract negotiations, and speak with the management, the orchestra, the theatrical director. He only saw to what concerned him personally. The wardrobe people, his dressing room, his make-up. All he was interested in was his costumes, his make-up and singing. The rest of the world had to revolve around him. We were in town for four days, and I saw him maybe three times, each time briefly. Oh, once I think we dined together, in that restaurant in Piedigrotta, the famous one. I remember it because he sent the fish back twice, he didn't like the way it was cooked. I can still see the look on the owner's face. What a bastard."

"What are the reasons behind your resentment? It seems to me that relations between you were particularly difficult and therefore not solely professional."

"It was impossible to have a good relationship with Arnaldo Vezzi. In fact, the only way to relate to him was to be a doormat and comply with everything he said. This might be acceptable, it's happened to me other times, but not under certain specific circumstances when the position becomes untenable."

Ricciardi leaned forwards slightly.

"For example?" he said.

"For example, when he got drunk in Berlin and showed up at the Chancellor's an hour late. Or when he was discovered in a hotel with a thirteen-year-old girl, the hotelkeeper's daughter. Or again when, in Vienna—in a fit of anger over what he said was a delayed opening bar—he smashed a fifty-thousand lira violin on the floor, after tearing it away from an orchestra player. Shall I go on?"

"So how did you keep up a professional relationship? On what basis?"

"Simple: on the grounds that he was a genius. An absolute genius. Apart from the voice, which was extraordinary, his feeling for the stage, his ability to perform any role perfectly, immersing himself in the character. And I mean becoming one with him: he donned the soul of the character he was playing, he identified with him completely. I have a theory: I think he was able to do it because he didn't have a soul of his own. So it was like writing on a clean slate, a tabula rasa; he had no feelings of his own to keep hidden. A snake."

"And so?"

"So there was no greater tenor in the world. Representing him was simply a matter of directing traffic. We could have had roles booked for ten years, if he had wanted to."

Ricciardi frowned, puzzled.

"But then his death is a serious loss to you, isn't it? You've lost an important client. If for no other reason than that, you should be grieving."

"No, Commissario. If you haven't already heard it from that imbecile, his secretary, I'll tell you myself: Vezzi had decided not to avail himself of my services anymore. He said, very magnanimously, as he always did, that he could command the same fees and save ten per cent besides. Sadly, I must admit that he was right."

"So, practically speaking, he had fired you."

"Practically speaking; but starting next season. I would still have gone on representing him until the end of this season. So all the complaints, the claims for penalties, the fines—they all still came to my office, unfortunately."

Ricciardi still wasn't quite clear.

"But the artistic decisions, the operas he would sing, the dates—did he coordinate them with you?"

"Who, Vezzi? It's obvious you didn't know him," Marelli said with a bitter smile. "Certainly that's how it should be and that's the way it is with all the other artists I represent. But not with Arnaldo. He did whatever he liked, whenever it occurred to him. Subject to later changing his mind and deciding otherwise, leaving dozens of people and their jobs hanging. Look,

Commissario, my only regret in this matter is missing the chance to see what would have happened next season, when Vezzi would have tried to manage on his own. Take my word for it, I'm sure he would have ended up paying twice his earnings, at least, in fines and penalties. Only I know the effort it cost me to try and repair the damage he caused."

"How come you agreed to represent him, if he was such a difficult personality?"

"Do you follow opera, Commissario? No? Well, let me explain something to you. My generation, let's say those now over forty, will remain hooked on opera forever. Like our parents and grandparents. Hooked on the passion, joy and sorrow we see onstage, whether from the gallery, the orchestra or, for those fortunate enough, the box seats. It was and is an opportunity to meet people, a way to acknowledge renowned, thrilling music.

'But things are changing: just look around. The radio, dance tunes. Jazz, the music of American Negroes. And especially movies. Have you had occasion to see a sound film yet? In Naples you have two sound theaters, I believe. In Milan there are already four, in Rome there are actually six. And sound films have been in Italy for only a year or so. People today want to act, not listen. It's no longer enough to sit and watch, or at most applaud or boo: they want to dance, sing along, whistle. They want to be part of the scene, watching the two stars kissing passionately, from up close. Or they want to go to the stadium and see twenty guys in shorts, working up a sweat. Where will that leave opera, in the future? Of less and less interest, I'm telling you. Less and less.

'That's why a Vezzi, when one comes along, must be safeguarded and protected. Because a talent like that only comes along once every century. Someone like Vezzi fills the theater, each time he sings. Even if he sings the same thing a hundred times over, people will go to hear him a hundred times. Why?

Because each time people hear something new, something different. A different marvel. So, better a Vezzi with all his temper tantrums and flaws, his nasty remarks and the humiliation he inflicts, than a thousand decent, conscientious professionals, hard-working and respectful of others' work, but without true talent. That type will always have a half-empty theater, mark Marelli's words; and Marelli has a certain experience, Signor Commissario."

Ricciardi nodded, his expression wry. He had already heard that speech.

"So then, in your opinion, who could have killed him?"

Marelli gave a brief, joyless laugh.

"Oh, just about anyone. Anyone who'd had a chance to see his vicious black soul, even for just a moment. I myself felt the urge to strangle him at least a thousand times. But who would strangle the goose that laid the golden egg? Not a businessman."

"Speaking of which, on the twenty-fifth you—"

"I was at La Scala, where they were performing *La Traviata*. Two of my artists were in it. Talented young men, serious professionals. They'll never fill the theater on their own, but those two will still be with me next year."

## XX

So, there's another one. Marelli too, Ricciardi thought when he found himself alone in his office, had excellent reasons for disliking Vezzi. And excellent reasons to keep him alive and in good health, at least until the end of the season. I wonder what life must be like, he thought, if you're surrounded by people who hate you, yet who depend on you. Maybe you'd think you were a malevolent deity, to whom the faithful offer sacrifices to ward off lightning or drought. Or maybe you'd feel lonely; even more lonely.

In any case, Marelli too had an alibi that could easily be verified: the theater. Ricciardi made a note and called Maione in.

"Verify Marelli's presence at La Scala on the twenty-fifth. Send a phonogram to the Questura in Milan. Is Signora Vezzi out there?"

"Yes, *Commissa'*. She hasn't raised her veil for a moment, and she hasn't said a word. She's sitting there, straight as a rod, not even looking around. It's a little unsettling, to tell the truth. Shall I send her in?"

"Yes, have her come in. You can even go home if you want to, I think we're done for today."

"Okay, *Commissa'*. Just in case, I'll wait until you're finished with the signora, should you need anything."

Ricciardi, noblesse oblige, waited for Signora Vezzi at the doorway to his office. He was therefore able to see her coming from the end of the hallway, where the waiting room was. Tall, wearing black, a coat with a fur collar, a hat with a veil that covered her face. He discerned a full, generous figure, though her walk was lithe and confident, not heavy. A compliant bearing, but tense. As if she might easily run off at any second.

She stopped in front of him a moment and tilted her head slightly to one side. The Commissario was aware of her gaze under the veil that concealed her features. He stood aside to let her enter; he held out a chair for her and, after she was seated, walked around the desk and sat down in turn. A wild fragrance, like spices, pervaded the room.

For a moment the woman was still. Then, with a slow, determined gesture, she raised her hands to her hat and took it off. A face with regular features, fair complexion. A hint of make-up accentuated full lips, large, dark eyes, a straight, not-quite-long nose; a well-proportioned oval, with a slight dimple on the chin. Signora Livia Lucani, now the widow Vezzi, was very beautiful and she knew it. She looked at the Commissario with curiosity, so different was he from what she had expected.

Seated across from her, his hands clasped before him, Ricciardi watched her face steadily, his eyes expressionless. He wondered what was behind that arrogant look of hers.

Pride, maybe. An echo of sorrow. But not a recent sorrow, not the death of her husband. Rather, something from further back. At times Ricciardi preferred the dead: they said the same thing over and over, but at least they spoke. The living, instead, just looked at you, and you had no idea what they were thinking. Especially women.

After a moment or two, though it seemed much longer to him, Ricciardi spoke.

"Signora, first of all I offer you my personal condolences along with those of the Questura. I want you to know that we will do everything in our power to ensure that the person who committed the crime is punished."

"Thank you, Commissario. Thank you very much. I'm sure you will."

Livia had a deep, modulated voice. Ricciardi thought it was natural, they'd told him that she had been a singer, a contralto. Still, he was surprised just the same. A low, rich sound. But also mellow, extremely feminine.

"You'll have to forgive me, Signora, for having to ask you certain questions. They are designed for the purpose I mentioned. But if it becomes too painful for you to answer, if you are tired from travelling or simply if your grief . . . what I mean is, I don't want to be intrusive. All you have to do is tell me, and we'll postpone the questioning."

"No, Commissario. My journey has been anything but tiring. Besides, now is the time and it can't be helped. Will I have to . . . see him? See my husband?"

The way she referred to him: there was a bit of fear in the woman's tone. Certainly not love, nor regret.

"I'm afraid so, for identification. You're his next of kin. It's the law. He's not here, however. He's at the hospital. We'll take you there tomorrow morning."

"How did it happen? I mean . . . they didn't tell me. How was he struck? Did they . . . disfigure him?"

Dread. Fear of not being able to face the horror. Ricciardi knew this feeling, he encountered it often. As if it hadn't been another human being who attacked. What should I tell you, Signora? About his final song of love that turns to hate? Or about the blood I can see gushing out of the pierced artery?

"No, Signora. A single wound, fatal, not to the face. Perhaps accidental, not intentionally inflicted. A scuffle. We don't know yet. But no disfigurement, no."

Livia brought a trembling gloved hand to her face. She didn't want to cry and she would not cry. She had exhausted her tears years ago. But she was afraid that seeing the corpse of the man whom she had once loved would be too much for her. Beyond that she couldn't help feeling intrigued by the man seated before her. Those steady green eyes, so strange in that dark face. The sharp nose, the nostrils quivering a little. The line of the eyebrows, slightly contracted at the centre, almost a natural scowl. The thin, tight lips, the instinctive twitch of the jaw. And that strand of hair over his face, like a boy, softening the overall impression of harshness. He reminded her of an unmounted emerald, cold and indifferent, but magnetic and compelling. She couldn't tear her eyes away.

Ricciardi, seemingly unaware of the woman's persistent observation, was studying her in turn, trying to get a sense of what she was feeling. If hunger and love, along with any variation of those needs, lay at the bottom of every crime, then a woman, a beautiful woman, could be the source of a motive. Though geographically distant, a wife could provoke displeasure, jealousy or envy and trigger all kinds of reactions. Ricciardi had seen many such women, and he knew that he would meet many more yet to come.

This one, moreover, was a woman who could drive any man crazy. Reading into those deep, expressive dark eyes, Ricciardi saw great vitality along with a profound intelligence and an awareness of her own beauty: a mixture more potent than any explosive.

"How long had it been since you'd seen your husband, Signora?"

"Three months, I believe. Not since Christmas, more or less."

Ricciardi stared at her.

"It doesn't seem normal, does it? I know. But my family was never a normal one. With Arnaldo it wasn't possible to be a family. He . . . well . . . he should have remained single. In actuality, our entire marriage was expedient for him. For his career. Not to mention that, in these times, you can't have a career, public visibility, without a beautiful family. And so, you need a marriage. A beautiful public marriage."

"And you, Signora? How was it expedient for you?"

Livia did not seem to notice the sarcasm in Ricciardi's voice. She was gazing straight ahead, unseeing, following the thread of memories.

"Expedient? The advantage of marrying a genius, the greatest of all time. And the man you love. Whom you think you love. Or whom you once loved, perhaps. Are you married, Commissario?"

"No. I'm not. What is it like to be married? Explain it to me, Signora."

"I don't know. During all those years, I don't recall ever feeling that he was mine. The house, of course: the furniture, the social events. The important people, the Party, the people in power. Paintings, sculptures. Awards. Travelling, smiling for the press, the flashbulbs. Aeroplanes, even. Sleeping cars. More smiles. But only outside the walls. At home, it meant waiting alone. Waiting for what?"

"And him? He, meanwhile?"

Still staring into space, Livia recalled the loneliness.

"He was always on the go. I protested when he came back, I asked him to explain. How dare you? he would say. 'Remember your role. I have to live, I am the great Vezzi. Let me live, let me go.' And love . . . "

"And love?"

"Love dies. The arms that held you tight become barriers that keep you out. The face that you caressed with your eyes, in sleep, becomes the sign of your end. As well as the end of your aspirations, of your career. I was talented, did you know that, Commissario? Truly talented. I sang in New York, in London. Even here at the San Carlo, in 1922, I performed in *L'italiana in Algeri*. But then I sacrificed it all on the altar of the great god Vezzi. I don't know why he married me, why it was me he wanted. I've asked myself that question hundreds, thousands of times over the years. He could have had anyone he wanted, women of title, heiresses to great wealth, but he wanted me. I was engaged to a Florentine count when we were introduced, but he paid no attention whatsoever. He started courting me, showering me with roses, letters, messages; he seemed obsessed. I saw him get like that on other occasions, afterwards: it's how he was. When he wanted something, anything, he couldn't sleep, he couldn't live until he got it. That's how it was with me."

Ricciardi listened intently. He was looking for the seed of revenge in Livia's words, but he didn't find it.

"But don't you feel bitter or angry, over your life? Don't you feel robbed of something that belonged to you?"

The woman looked up and found herself staring into those green eyes. She drowned in them, for a long moment that stretched out markedly. She saw in them a familiarity with suffering, she recognized a sense of sorrow.

"Have you lost someone, Commissario? Did you ever lose someone you loved dearly?"

For a moment Ricciardi said nothing. He saw again the man in the park at San Martino, the yellowish foam bubbling out of his mouth, his hands tightly gripping his stomach as he kept saying, "*I can't live without you*," while the woman hanging from a tree asked, "*Why, my love?*" over and over again.

"Let's say I'm familiar with this kind of loss, I've seen many such cases in my work, and I know about absence."

"Well then, if you know about absence, you know that it becomes a condition. You get used to it, if you survive. I got used to it. Six years ago I had Arnaldo's child. I thought I would recapture the signs of joy and lost love. But it was not to be. The same God who had sentenced me to life imprisonment took away the joy that He had given me. Is it better to be blind from birth or to become blind? Not to know colours or at least be able to remember them? I asked myself that too, a thousand times. All these years, always asking myself the same questions."

"What happened to the baby?"

"He died of diphtheria, at the age of one. Arnaldo wouldn't forgive me, as if I had killed him. 'You weren't even able to be a mother,' he told me. He needed a son as much as he needed a wife; even more so. Continuity, succession. Then too, a proof of virility, of the quality of his seed, to offer the Party, the nation. Such idiocy. Don't you think it's sheer idiocy, Commissario? Or are you one of those who believe in these things?"

"No, I'm not one of those. And then? What happened afterwards? You never grew close again?"

Livia sighed, running a hand through her hair.

"No. But then we were never close. Besides, if a child brings you together, losing him can tear you apart completely. Assuming our marriage ever existed."

She paused to follow a thought. Then she looked directly into Ricciardi's eyes.

"Have you ever seen a ghost, Commissario?"

"Who knows. Perhaps, at times. But maybe we all see them."

"I live with the ghost of my child. He keeps me company, I talk to him. I think I see him, sometimes. I feel him in my arms, I feel his weight."

"And your husband? What happened, afterwards?"

"He went his own way, once and for all. He no longer even tried to keep up appearances. We'd see each other at official events, and I went to hear him sing a couple of times. He had his affairs, I had mine. No apologies, not anymore."

Ricciardi raised an eyebrow.

"Your affairs?"

Livia lifted her chin, proudly.

"I'm a woman: mortally wounded, but still alive. I needed to feel appreciated, yes. To see if I was still able to attract a glance, a smile. If I might still receive a bouquet of roses, a love letter. Besides, was I supposed to remain faithful? To whom? To a man who didn't come home for months? And who didn't think twice about humiliating me, appearing in public with other women? You should have seen it, the commiseration on the faces of our friends, our important acquaintances. Maybe I too was hoping to hurt him a little."

"Forgive me, Signora. I didn't mean to offend you; these are matters that don't concern me. It was to see if there might be someone who for some reason wanted to get rid of your husband. To have you for himself, perhaps."

"No, Commissario. I haven't been seeing anyone for months. You can easily verify it. I spent all week in Pesaro, at my parents' house. Alone. As always."

When she said goodbye to Ricciardi, Livia turned and, before lowering the veil over her face, unexpectedly smiled at him. A radiant, very tender smile. She tilted her head to the side and gave him a long meaningful look.

"I'm staying at the Excelsior, Commissario. Should you need me for anything further, send for me. In any case, I will be here tomorrow morning to identify the body at the hospital."

# XXI

Ricciardi found that Maione had not yet left, so he asked him to accompany Livia to her hotel. But he also asked him to check with the Questura in Pesaro, to verify the woman's continued presence during that period and whether she was really alone.

Then he decided to go home. He was cold.

Along the way he tried to bring some order to the facts and details he'd acquired during that long day of interrogations. He felt a familiar sense of uneasiness: like when you've forgotten to do something, or lost a certain item, or haven't considered a particular aspect. Someone had said something important, something essential, and he couldn't seem to bring that something to a conscious level, to be able to use it. But who? And what was it?

The wind had picked up again, blowing relentlessly; the only sounds along the deserted street were the banging of a shutter, the clatter of a horse's hooves on the cobblestones and the wind howling in the doorways. His *tata* had prepared his supper and was waiting for him, sewing something for some distant relative in Fortino. When she saw him she began airing her usual concerns.

"A new case, eh? Another murder. I can tell right away—your face changes. You become obsessed. When a man works, he works. But when he's home, he should think about himself. Not you though, always thinking about murdered bodies, blood and knives. Why don't you think about starting a family instead? They're imposing a tax now, those who aren't married have to pay it. What are you going to do, pay a tax? What is it that you don't have? You could catch the best woman in Naples, with your good looks and your wealth. And you're still young. You think you'll be young forever? To me it seems like just yesterday that I was a beautiful *guagliona* and now I'm a decrepit old lady. And who did I spend my whole life looking after? A man who doesn't even want to have children! Not even a scrap of satisfaction for this poor little old woman. It's shameful!"

Ricciardi, resigned to the background sounds of Rosa's grumbling, went on eating as he reflected. He had delineated Vezzi's personality, there was no doubt about that. A disreputable, dreadful individual, the quintessence of the worst a man could be. Gifted with an incomparable talent and the appeal that brought with it. But who was attracted by that appeal? Those who were part of his world, which in fact he never ventured out of. Yet he had a beautiful wife, and one who, at the beginning, was in love with him. Is it possible he hadn't understood the tragedy his wife had experienced when she lost her baby? No question about it, Livia was beautiful; on that score there could be no doubt. Even he, who normally paid little attention to these things, had been aware of it. Captivating; there was something feline about her. Certainly not reassuring.

" . . . A nice quiet woman. Someone who will take care of you when I die—which, if you ask me, will be soon seeing how these old bones of mine ache. God knows the effort it takes to keep up this house. And then the washing and ironing, hanging the clothes out to dry, sewing on the buttons you're always losing. And preparing supper that ends up getting cold because you never come home in the evening. What kind of a life is that?"

Can a man go so far as to kill for a woman? He had seen men

kill for much less than Livia's eyes, her perfume. But who could have entered the area of the dressing rooms during the performance? An outsider would have attracted everyone's attention, but someone who was part of the surroundings, part of the theater, could have gone unnoticed. Entered, then left the dressing room? How? Ricciardi smiled distractedly at Rosa, kissed her on the forehead and went off to his room.

The sea was roaring on the rocks, driven by the wind. From the third-floor window of the Hotel Excelsior towering sprays of greyish foam could be seen in the darkness, along with fishing boats anchored far from shore, bobbing wildly in the waves. In the shadows of her room, Livia smoked as she watched the storm-tossed scene.

She could have gone out. Marelli, Arnaldo's manager, had invited her to dinner. He had hinted that, now, she could even go back to singing; that Vezzi's name would no longer be an obstacle but would, on the contrary, offer excellent exposure. That, now, the hurdle of being in the great tenor's shadow no longer existed. Now. The key word was "now." Now she was free.

But did Livia feel free? Or would she see another ghost now? His breath, his hands. Arnaldo's voice. The man he was at the beginning, the man he had become at the end. Maybe it could not have been any different, for a man like him. She was afraid to see the body: afraid that it might not be him after all.

She didn't know why she had spoken about him today with the Commissario. It had been a long time, she thought, inhaling the smoke, since she had talked to anyone about him. Even her parents, always solicitous and there for her, who since Carletto's death called her "poor Livia", hadn't heard her speak of Arnaldo for years. Nor did they ask about him, having certainly understood the situation. Yet today, in front of a stranger and at such a grave time, she had revealed her most secret emotions.

Livia recalled what she had sensed in Ricciardi: that he was resigned to suffering. The suffering of others, which he had made his own and which had become a way of life. It wasn't hard for her to admit that she was attracted by that man, by his cold, expressionless eyes. She had turned down Marelli's dinner invitation, it would have to be another time. Her career had waited this long, it could wait another night.

She smiled bitterly, in the darkness, thinking about those green eyes. Outside, the wind and sea howled.

In the warm, brightly lit kitchen, Enrica was cleaning up after dinner with her family. The usual chaos reigned, as if a battalion of hungry mercenaries had passed through.

Sounds came from the other rooms: her sisters and brother making a racket, her baby nephew crying, her father arguing with her mother, sister and brother-in-law. Enrica didn't mind straightening up after supper, patiently and doggedly. Her mild, stubborn nature found its chief expression in being orderly. She didn't want any help and smilingly declined the offers of her mother, who had arthritis, and her younger sister, who had the small child to think of. All she asked was that they stay out of the kitchen and let her take her time. This was her little kingdom. That's how Enrica was: calm, smiling and not very talkative. Not turning around, she glanced towards the window. Still nothing.

That evening the voices of the adults were rather excited. Politics, she thought. Always politics. As the years passed and the regime became more entrenched, people's views grew further and further apart. Enrica's father, a liberal, was convinced that freedom was being progressively eroded; that it was difficult for those who saw things differently from the majority to express their opinion without incurring some act of violence. That the economy was stagnating, as evidenced by the fact that his daughter and son-in-law, with their baby, were forced to continue living with them instead of on their own.

But her brother-in-law, a clerk in his father-in-law's shop, and an enthusiastic member of the Fascist Party, retorted that this was a defeatist attitude; you had to have faith in the decisions of *Il Duce* and the hierarchies who would do what was good for the country; and sacrifices had to be made now in order to be unsurpassed in the world in the future. Because that was Italy's destiny, since the time of Rome: to predominate, for the good of mankind. They should feel proud to be Italian, and accept those sacrifices confidently. Once that destiny was fulfilled, there would be prosperity and well-being.

Enrica hated to hear them arguing. But she knew they loved each other and that this dispute too would end with a glass of cognac, in front of the radio. As far as she was concerned, she didn't know what to make of the subject: she seemed to think her father was right, yet she had the feeling that this did not make him happy. She glanced briefly at the window. Still nothing.

She herself, she knew, was a cause of concern for her parents. She felt it more and more often in her mother's caresses, in her father's sighs when he looked at her; her younger sister had been married for over a year after a five-year engagement. For some time now she had been turning down invitations from her girlfriends, who wanted her to come dancing with them on Saturday afternoons. Enrica wasn't beautiful; she was tall, wore glasses for myopia, she wasn't particularly graceful in her movements, and her legs were too long. Still, she had an extraordinary way of smiling, tilting her head to the side and lowering her eyes, and several young men had asked her sisters and girlfriends about her. Politely and quietly, though not allowing any objections, she would refuse the invitation without offending anyone. She liked to read, to embroider. To listen to music on the radio. Romantic music, the kind that made you dream. Sometimes she went to the movies and she had even seen a 'talkie' a few months earlier; enthralled by the sound, she had wept. Her father, touched by it, had teased her a little. She put a plate in the cabinet, near the window. She looked out. Nothing yet.

She kept the truth to herself. She didn't want to tell anyone how, in her heart, she didn't feel free to accept the young men's overtures. Oh, she knew they would laugh. They would say she was the usual naïve dreamer, that reality was a different matter. The reality was that she was twenty-four years old and still single. That it was pointless to embroider a trousseau that in all likelihood would never be put to use. That if she wanted a family with children and a house, she'd better get a social life, without wasting any time.

But there was more she would also have to tell, for the sake of completeness: about the window opposite and the curtains that opened every evening, though not always at the same time; about that moment at the street vendor's cart, when she'd found herself looking into the most desperate eyes that she had ever seen in her life. How every night she felt those same feverish eyes on her, for hours. From behind a windowpane in winter, and unobstructed in summer, when the scent of the sea reached Santa Teresa, borne by the hot wind from the south. And how that gaze was everything, a promise, a dream, even an ardent embrace. Thinking about it, she instinctively turned to the window. The curtain opposite was open. Lowering her eyes and blushing, Enrica hid a small smile: good evening, my love.

Ricciardi watched Enrica. He enjoyed her slow, methodical, precise movements.

Something was missing: a detail, some aspect. He was certain that he was close to a solution, or at least to the path that would lead to the solution. A phrase: a phrase that he had heard, that he had filed away in a corner of his memory and no longer remembered.

Enrica was stacking the dishes in the sink carefully, from the smallest to the largest.

The facts, let's see, from the smallest to the largest. He remembered the important ones easily, no need to concentrate. Focus on the seemingly insignificant ones.

Enrica wiped the table clean with a dishcloth.

Let's go over the things they said: who did I talk to first?

Enrica arranged the chairs around the kitchen table.

Don Pierino, who described the operas' plots.

Enrica folded the dishcloth, after shaking it out.

The priest had also talked about Vezzi, about how great he was. His voice had actually trembled.

Enrica was now sweeping the floor, clearing away the crumbs from supper.

He remembered don Pierino's excitement, yet the Assistant Pastor had not seen the rehearsals; he had been specific about that.

Enrica had finished straightening up and looked around, satisfied.

Don Pierino had said that he had heard the voice on recordings and in other performances. Not this time, however.

Enrica was getting her embroidery box; she would move the chair near the window and turn on the lamp. It was the brightest moment of Ricciardi's day: seeing her sitting there as she began embroidering with her left hand, her head slightly tilted to one side. It made his heart tremble.

Don Pierino telling him: "Seeing him up close, yesterday, made my heart tremble."

In the darkness of the bedroom an extraordinary thing happened: the sombre Commissario Ricciardi, in his flannel robe, hairnet on his head, smiled and said, in a whisper: "Thank you. Goodnight, my love."

# XXII

Don Pierino elevated the Host above his head, during the consecration. More than any other act it was the one that made him feel closest to God, a mediator between Him and mankind, the one who would attain a morsel of paradise to bestow on the community. That was the reason he had become a priest.

He bowed before the altar, resting his forehead on the white linen cloth that covered the marble. Outside, the wind howled its lament, the voice of another creature.

When he raised his eyes, don Pierino saw, in the dim light of seven in the morning, a familiar figure standing at the back of the church.

The man was bareheaded, but he was not holding a hat. He had his hands in his coat pockets, his legs slightly apart, a strand of hair falling over his face. Leaving the sacristy after removing the sacred vestments, don Pierino found him there waiting for him.

"Commissario! What brings you here, may I ask?"

Ricciardi smiled wryly.

"Already so cheerful this early in the morning, Father? A good breakfast, or the help of faith?"

"Faith, evidently; I haven't had breakfast yet. Won't you join me, Commissario? Milk and coffee in the sacristy?"

"Coffee and *biscotti*, but across the street at Gambrinus. I'm buying."

"Of course you're buying. Vow of poverty, remember?"

Outside, the city had awakened. A team of labourers, in work clothes, waited for the trolley to leave for the steel mill in Bagnoli. Several schoolgirls, in black smocks and capes, were making their way towards the day school in Piazza Dante. Carriages and taxis were beginning to gather in Piazza del Plebiscito, awaiting the businessmen who would soon flood the streets. Masons, in groups of three or four, were setting off for the waterfront where the street was being paved with asphalt.

"Father, I came to ask you something. Yesterday morning you told me that you had not heard Vezzi sing this time; is that right?"

"That's right, Commissario. When he was there, the doors were kept strictly closed during rehearsals. Moreover, he only attended the dress rehearsal. Then, the other night, as you know, he didn't have a chance to sing."

Ricciardi leaned across the table.

"And yet, I remember you said you saw him up close, the day before yesterday, you were very excited. Did I misunderstand you?"

Don Pierino smiled sadly.

"No, Commissario, you understood correctly. In fact, now that I think of it, I may have been among the last to see him alive, except for whoever killed him, of course."

"Under what circumstances? Please, Father, it's very important that you tell me all the details."

"Oh, it's quite simple. I was in the famous niche, at the top of the stairs leading from the garden entrance to the dressing rooms. I must have inadvertently stepped back, it's not a very big space, believe me, and backed into the hallway. Then I felt someone bump into me somewhat forcefully and I faltered a bit. I turned around and saw this enormous, tall, heavyset man. He said "Excuse me" and I said "Excuse *me,*" or something like that. As you know, I shouldn't have been there. And then I saw him enter Vezzi's dressing room, under the flight of stairs."

Ricciardi's eyes, unblinking, were fixed on the priest's face with the utmost concentration.

"What did he look like, Father? How was he dressed, how did you recognize him?"

Don Pierino strained to recall the exact details.

"He was wearing an overcoat, a long, black coat. And a white wool scarf that nearly covered his entire face. A black, broad-brimmed hat, pulled down almost over his eyes. No, I hardly saw the face. But it was Vezzi, I'm sure of it. Otherwise, why would he enter that dressing room?"

Right, Ricciardi thought. Why indeed?

Her fragrance reached him first. Ricciardi looked up from the report he was writing, struck by the heady, distinctive wild scent of spices. A second before he connected the perfume to the person, Maione stuck his head in the door.

"*Commissa'*, Signora Vezzi is here."

Ricciardi asked him to show her in and Livia entered the office. She wore a sober black suit, the mid-length skirt hugging the supple lines of her hips. The jacket, buttoned to the neck, enclosed an ample though not overstated bosom. She carried the fur-collared coat on her arm, her handbag slung over her shoulder. Her hat, tilted slightly sideways, had its black veil raised. Her face bore no signs of what, Ricciardi imagined, must not have been a restful night. The large dark eyes were bright and alert, the light make-up softening her expression. The full lips assumed a faint smile.

"The way I left you, that's how I find you, Commissario. Don't you leave the office at night?"

Maione, who had remained standing in the doorway, raised an eyebrow.

"Physically, yes, Signora. But only physically. How are you? Do you feel up to it?"

"Certainly, Commissario. That's why I came; as difficult as it may be."

Ricciardi instructed Maione to call for one of the Questura's three cars and to notify Dr. Modo that they were on their way to the hospital to identify the body.

The brief ride took place in silence. Maione drove, something which did not come very naturally to him. His imprecations against unexpected obstacles were the only words uttered in the car.

Livia had lowered her veil and was breathing softly; she could feel Ricciardi's presence beside her, his tension palpable. The Commissario was thinking about the information he had obtained from don Pierino shortly before. It was clear that the man who had bumped into the priest was not Vezzi. First, because by that time the tenor must already have been dead. And then because Vezzi would surely have been wearing his make-up and the scarf would therefore have been smeared with greasepaint; instead it was spotless. But then, why come back in? Once having fled through the window, why not melt away in the dark rather than risk being seen? And finally, how could the killer be sure that the corpse had not been discovered in the meantime? Still too many murky aspects. But Ricciardi was convinced that he had scored an important point in the match against the murderer.

At the hospital, in the mortuary, they found Dr. Modo in his white coat. The medical examiner was visibly struck by Livia's statuesque beauty, as he offered his condolences.

"Thank you, Doctor. I wish I could say that I am inconsolably saddened. Instead, I feel a dull regret; a kind of melancholy. Nostalgia for a bygone time, perhaps. But no sorrow."

"I'm sorry, Signora. I'm very sorry. There is nothing sadder than dying without leaving any sorrow."

Ricciardi stood aside, listening to them. He thought about the tears running down the clown's face, tracing two dark lines in the white greasepaint. He saw his half-closed eyes, his slightly bent legs, he heard the words of his final song. Of course there had been sorrow: the sorrow of loss, the sorrow of someone being robbed of years and years yet to be lived.

An attendant pushed the stretcher holding the body, which was covered with a white sheet. They took their places, Livia and Ricciardi on one side, Modo on the other. The doctor lifted the edge of the sheet covering the face of the rag doll that had been a man: all three remained silent, studying the waxen face. Their eyes ran from the small swelling on the cheekbone, the size of a small coin, to the gash on the right side of the neck. The eyes and mouth were slightly parted, as if the corpse were feeling a subtle pleasure, as if he were hearing a music heard only by him. In the centre of the throat, the incision resulting from the autopsy, closed with cross-stitches.

"It's him," Livia breathed out, her tightly clasped hands white from being gripped so hard. Ricciardi took one hand from his coat pocket and slipped it under the woman's arm; she leaned on it so as not to fall.

"I'm sorry," she said. "I thought I was prepared. I thought about it a great deal. But maybe it's not possible to prepare oneself, is it?"

The doctor sighed, faced with a situation that was all too familiar to him. He covered the body again and nodded to the attendant who stood waiting nearby. The man wheeled away the stretcher and no one ever saw Arnaldo Vezzi again in the flesh.

In the small room opposite the mortuary, the doctor offered Livia a cigarette, which she lit with trembling hands.

"How absurd. Such greatness, so many dreams. The magic of an incomparable voice. The hubris, the omnipotence. Then, all this silence."

Dr. Modo sighed.

"That's always the way, Signora. Regardless of who the person was. The same dignity, the same silence. Whether it's war or illness. No matter how many people are out here waiting, in there they are always alone, in silence."

Ricciardi listened and thought about it. Silence, did you say, Doctor? You can't imagine how much they still have to say. They sing, laugh. Talk. Shout. Only you can't hear them. It has to do with the ear: they emit a sound that you don't hear. But I hear it. Loud and clear.

Livia thanked the doctor, and he told her to consider him at her disposal. Retrieving the body, for the funeral: Marelli, the manager, would see to it. Etcetera, etcetera. The unvarying rhetoric of death.

The return trip was different. Livia was noticeably relieved, for a number of reasons. She was beginning to realize that an important chapter of her life was in any event closed. In that city that wasn't hers, lashed by that strange, unseasonably cold wind, she had perhaps regained the freedom that she had stopped searching for years ago. Even Arnaldo's face, harrowed by death, no longer seemed hateful; she thought that perhaps in time she would be able to remember the few positive things about him, the happy moments from the time they had met and the early years of their marriage.

"Do you believe in fate, Commissario?"

"No, Signora. I don't. I believe in people and their emotions. In love, hate. Hunger. Sorrow, above all."

He looked steadily straight ahead as he spoke, his head sunk between his shoulders, huddled in the upturned collar of his overcoat. Livia observed his sharp profile, the rebellious strand of hair falling over his face. She sensed his remoteness, as if he were speaking from another world or from another time.

Maione drove in silence, not even cursing the urchins who ran into the street barefoot, chasing a ball of rags or newspaper, propelled by the wind. He was studying the Commissario in the rear-view mirror, surprised by his words: he had never heard that tone, so rapt in thought.

The woman went on. "Well then? In your opinion, how many chances does a person have in his life, to construct a little happiness?"

"As many as he wants, Signora. Maybe none. But illusions, those for sure. Every day even, every moment. Illusions though. Only illusions."

Livia saw that Ricciardi's mind wasn't with them, that it was wandering elsewhere. So she fell silent, until they reached the Questura.

When they got there Maione asked the signora if she needed a ride to the hotel. The woman said she would prefer to walk a little, even in that wind; she needed some air. She approached Ricciardi.

"Commissario, for the moment I will remain in the city. I don't feel like going home just now. I'll wait for the investigation to be completed, if it doesn't take too long. You know the name of my hotel. Should you need me, you know where to find me."

"Of course, Signora. I'll keep it in mind, I assure you."

Another hint fallen on deaf ears. Livia thought of the many times when a smile or a word had been enough to encourage someone. She didn't know why those eyes, that voice, troubled her so; and she didn't know how to make Ricciardi understand that she would have liked to meet him, to talk about something other than her husband's murder.

She decided to be more direct.

"What is it, Commissario? There always seem to be two dialogues between us: a spoken one and an unspoken one. Why don't things work with you the way they do with other men? Maybe you have no feelings?"

Maione, a few yards away, had a coughing fit. Ricciardi replied drily: "I wish, Signora. I would live a more peaceful life. But you have your sorrow and you should look for another port to shelter you from the storm."

Livia stood there looking at him. The wind fluttered the veil of her elegant hat. The deep dark eyes filled with tears which the sight of her dead husband had not aroused. She turned and walked away.

# XXIII

When they reached the office, Ricciardi told Maione that he needed to speak with don Pierino, the theater director and Bassi again. The secretary, by now clearly worried, was the first to arrive.

"Good morning, Commissario. Forgive me, but frankly I'm beginning to be puzzled by your continuing to summon me. I've told you everything I know. What more do you need from me?"

"Do you have something to hide, Signor Bassi? If so, then I suggest you speak up. Otherwise all you have to do is answer our questions honestly, now and whenever we need you to, and you'll have nothing to fear."

The man sighed, his shoulders hunched, his expression resigned.

"Of course, of course. I have nothing to hide, God forbid! What do you want to know?"

"Let's talk about Christmas. About the trip to Naples around December twentieth. I want to know Vezzi's movements during that time, or at least those you know about."

"Well let's see. We left the morning of the twentieth, and we arrived late that night. We came from Milan. Signor Marelli, the manager, was with us. We were to return the evening of the twenty-first: all we had to do was settle the terms of the contract, take a look at the set designs, get fitted for the costumes, things like that. Instead, we left later than we intended, on the night of the twenty-third; we nearly spent Christmas in Naples. I remember changing the ticket reservations twice."

Ricciardi listened intently. "How come, why the changes?"

"Oh, I haven't the faintest idea. The Maestro decided it. As usual he didn't say why. All we could do was accept it and adjust our plans accordingly."

"But did it have to do with the theater? That is, matters concerning the staging maybe, the orchestra . . . "

Bassi gave a nervous little laugh and adjusted his glasses on his nose.

"The theater, not a chance! He was only there on the morning of the twenty-first. A distracted glance at the set designs, a few words with the theater director, the costume fitting with wardrobe, then he disappeared for three days. No, Commissario, take my word for it: the theater had nothing to do with it. It was a different matter. Affairs of the heart, if you ask me. Not that I have any proof, of course."

"And where did he go?"

"I don't know. He came back to the hotel late at night and went to bed without even saying hello, as he usually did. Signor Marelli and I spent two days playing cards in the lounge of the Vesuvio."

Bassi had nothing more to say and was told he could go. Ricciardi was thinking; Maione broke the silence.

"I can verify the ticket changes and the actual travel times for all three of them at the railway station. The theater director isn't here yet: maybe he wants to make you wait to show how important he is. Should I tell you, as soon as he gets here?"

"Definitely. By all means go to the station."

The Brigadier hesitated, his hand on the doorknob. "*Commissa'*, if I may . . . there's something I'd like to say."

"Tell me. What is it?"

"I've been working with you for three years now. As you know . . . since Luca . . . my son . . . In short, during this time I've come to care about you. It's true that no one wants to work with you: they say you're not human, actually. Because you don't talk much, you're distant, and you work too hard: you never stop until you find out who did it. But I like working this way. It's what makes our work unlike other jobs."

"So?"

Maione hesitated, but he was determined to finish the little speech he had prepared.

"So, no one thinks more of you than I do and no one knows better than me how you put your heart and soul into your work. Still . . . you're over thirty, but you could be my son. I've lost my own son, and sometimes I look at you and think how skilled you are and, deep down, good as gold. I can feel it. I know it. But you're alone, *Commissa'*. And alone, we die. If I hadn't had my wife and children, these past few years, I would have died a hundred times over. Our work gradually expands, and little by little it can fill our entire life, like a cellar when it gets flooded. It's a mistake."

Ricciardi heard him out in silence. Perhaps he should have reproached him for getting too personal, but the Brigadier's enormous discomfiture moved him to pity. The man was red-faced, rubbing his foot on the floor, staring at his clasped hands. Ricciardi decided to let him continue.

"I talk about it sometimes with my wife. She knows you, she remembers you, you know, from the funeral. You paid your respects to her. And we both say it's a shame that a man like you is alone. Always working. And I thought, sometimes, you know, there are men who don't like women, who aren't interested in them. I thought that you, no offence, *Commissa'*, might be that way. But today, with that signora. Holy Mother of God, what a beauty! And with her husband just dead and all, though he was a bastard, we've heard that from everyone. So then, like a father to a son . . . You can even say to me, 'Maione, how dare you! Mind your own business.' But if I hadn't spoken up just now, and told you, I'd have it on my conscience. Take half a day off, *Commissa'*, and take the signora out to eat!"

He took a deep, liberating breath, like someone who's lifted a weight off his chest. Ricciardi stood up from his chair and went over to him. He put his hand on the Brigadier's arm as he had the day he told him that his son had died with his father's name on his lips.

"On the contrary, I thank you. I know you care about me and, in my own way, I care about you, too. I apologize for being brusque at times: I have a strange personality. But believe me, I'm fine the way I am. And give my regards to your wife."

Maione looked into his eyes for a moment, smiled and left.

The theater director Spinelli was quite agitated, as usual. He entered the office like a fury, stopped suddenly, and looked around.

"Here I am. I came immediately. Good day, Commissario. Is there anything new? I should be kept informed about the status of the investigation. After all, I feel that my position gives me certain rights in this regard."

As always, Ricciardi was more abrupt than he needed to be. He felt it was the right approach to keep someone like that at bay.

"When we have news, you'll know it, Director. For now, simply answer the questions I'm about to ask you."

Once again, Ricciardi's harshness had the power to silence the theater director, who assumed his usual air of indignation.

"I am at your disposition, Commissario."

"Last December, Vezzi came to the city with Bassi and Marelli to finalize contractual details for the performance of *Pagliacci*. Is that correct?"

"Of course, it's all recorded. I keep an up-to-date engagement book, should I have to account for my work at the Royal Theater. I remember it clearly. They arrived on the evening of the twentieth, we had been expecting them since morning but that was nothing new with Vezzi. They came to the theater on the twenty-first, and stayed the entire morning."

"Did they speak with you?"

"I welcomed all three, as is my duty. Then I lingered with Marelli to see to the administrative issues, let's say. Vezzi and Bassi, on the other hand, were with the stage manager, the wardrobe people and the production director, looking over the sketches, being fitted for costumes, things like that. They left at lunchtime."

"Do you remember any episode, anything out of the ordinary?"

"No. I only recall that a small crowd of stagehands, singers and orchestra players had gathered, having learned that he had come. Vezzi was a true legend in these circles. They wanted to meet him, to get his autograph. He got irritated and insisted on being left alone. He only met with the people I mentioned earlier."

"And then?"

The theater director looked at him, raising an eyebrow somewhat arrogantly.

"Didn't you hear me? They left, before one o'clock. They even refused my invitation to lunch together. I don't even know when they left the city."

## XXIV

A plausible dynamic of events was taking shape in Ricciardi's mind. Not so much the facts—too many loose ends still eluded him—as the emotions that had been generated. That was the way he worked: he created a scheme, a geography of the emotions he encountered. What he was able to gather from the Incident, the feelings of the individuals he questioned, the surprise, the horror of those present. Then he tried to piece together the victim's soul—its dark and light sides—from the words and looks of the people who had known him.

He didn't elaborate on the witnesses' words: there was the risk of remembering them wrong and, in any case, taken out of the context in which they were said they lost their meaning, their importance. Instead his memory focused on the speaker's attitude, his expression and passion: on the emotion that emerged, and above all that which remained beneath the surface. All told, he sensed rather than heard.

In Vezzi's murder, his being surprised by death, he sensed a single violent urge that was nonrecurring. An isolated wave of hatred, purposeful and clear, leaving destruction on the shore as it receded. And he sensed the clown caught off guard, with his last doleful song. But Ricciardi also felt that the song's words and its tone were discordant: that the victim's mood was one of sorrow and regret, whereas his song spoke of vengeance.

Over time he had learned that the Incident could also lead him off course in solving a crime. One time a murdered girl's final words had concerned her father and the investigation had proceeded in that direction. But the father she was referring to was a priest, and the man who ended up in jail was not the killer. Since then he tried to consider whatever meaning words might offer, without ruling anything out.

It was because of this dissonance, the jarring note he sensed between the song's words and the emotion, that he had summoned don Pierino again. He didn't know if it was the opera expert he wanted to meet with or the father confessor, capable of understanding people's souls though with parameters quite different from his own.

When Maione brought in the priest, Ricciardi stood up to greet him.

"Thank you for coming so quickly, Father. I really need to talk with you."

The priest, as always, smiled.

"My dear Commissario. I have already told you that for me it is a pleasure to be of help to you. How are things going?"

"Not particularly well, I'm afraid. I think I understand a few things, but there are still a few points that are obscure to me. Talk to me, Father. Tell me about *Pagliacci* and this character that Vezzi was playing. Canio, right?"

Don Pierino settled back in his chair and clasped his hands over his belly, raising his eyes to the window that was rattled by the wind.

"Canio, yes. The raging clown. Well then, the original drama about jealousy is, as you know, *Othello*. Verdi's music, Boito's libretto based on Shakespeare's tragedy. The Moor of Venice, you recall. There we have a crescendo of emotions, culminating in Othello's suicide after he has smothered Desdemona for her presumed infidelity. In reality, Desdemona is innocent. It was all a scheme contrived by Iago, the traitor.

"In *Pagliacci*, as in *Cavalleria Rusticana*, things are different: the woman is guilty, there actually is infidelity. It's a betrayal between a man and a woman, it's real, part of everyday life and, as Tonio says in the prologue, it can happen to anyone. There's nothing strange about it, nothing exotic. There are no riches, no soldiers, no gondolas or doges."

Ricciardi listened with the greatest attention, looking steadily at the priest.

"So, Canio, although he's a clown, is certainly not a cheerful character."

"Exactly, Commissario. In fact, if I may say so, I think the character Canio is one of the saddest of any opera. A man condemned to make people laugh, who instead is obsessed with not appearing ridiculous. It is hearing himself reminded by Beppe, Arlecchino, to perform, while he's suffering from jealousy, that finally makes him lose control."

"And, onstage, he kills his wife and her lover."

"Exactly. Here too there is a traitor, Tonio, the hunchback clown. His deformity represents wickedness, malice. But actually—though it's for selfish reasons, because he has designs on Canio's wife—he tells the truth: Nedda, Colombina, does have a lover. And that's the beauty of the libretto, the real drama takes place right onstage, the province of fiction. Almost as if to say that life always comes through, in the street, in the home, and even onstage."

"So Canio kills Tonio and Nedda?"

Don Pierino laughed.

"No, no! Nedda's lover isn't Tonio. It's Silvio, remember? I told you about him earlier. A young man from the village, not one of the troupe. Canio kills Nedda and then Silvio when he climbs onstage to help the woman."

"So the lover doesn't perform with Canio. Is that right?"

"Yes, exactly. He's a character who is not particularly significant, a baritone."

"And Canio, when he learns that Nedda really has a lover, goes mad with jealousy."

Don Pierino nodded, lost in thought.

"Yes; fiction and reality become confused. Canio plays the betrayed husband and, when he finds out the truth, he tears off his costume, singing '*No, pagliaccio non son!*'—no, I am not a clown—and then stabs his wife."

Ricciardi again saw the image of the clown in tears, blood gushing from the gash in his carotid artery, his hand outstretched, singing . . .

"*Io sangue voglio, all'ira m'abbandono . . .* "

" *. . . in odio tutto l'amor mio finì!*' don Pierino finished for him, clapping his hands and laughing delightedly. 'Bravo, Commissario! So you've been studying! Very nice, that quote, and particularly apropos, since the two operas are performed together. In fact, they tell the same story and the characters are closer than you might imagine."

Ricciardi looked at the priest, not following.

"Which characters, Father?"

"Canio and Alfio, of course! The lines you just recited, right?"

"But isn't it Canio who sings that in Pagliacci?"

"Are you pulling my leg? No, no, Alfio sings it in *Cavalleria Rusticana*. He too is a betrayed husband. They're his last lines as he leaves the stage, before the intermezzo. He sings them at the end of his duet with Santuzza, who reveals that his wife is betraying him with Turiddu, whom he kills in a duel at the end of the opera. But, if you didn't know . . . where did you hear it?"

Ricciardi was now staring into space, leaning slightly forwards in his chair. A whole new perspective had opened up, filling in many pieces of the puzzle.

"What was it you said before? The baritone . . . "

"Alfio is a baritone, yes. He has to have a deep voice, to reflect the hard work . . . "

"No, no, Father," Ricciardi raised a hand, interrupting him.

"What you said about the other baritone, Silvio: you said, 'a character who is not particularly significant.' Is that right?'

Don Pierino was confused. 'Yes, that's what I said. But he's not the one who sings the lines you quoted. Are you all right, Commissario? You look pale.'

"And who decides, in life, who is 'particularly significant'? Every man is particularly significant as far as he's concerned, isn't he, Father?'

Ricciardi seemed to be talking to himself, even though he addressed the priest.

"How many times, in the confessional, have you listened to the feelings and emotions of people 'not particularly significant'? Every day, from morning till night, I see the mayhem and delirium wrought by the emotions of people like that.'

Don Pierino protested vigorously.

"But I'm not referring to real people! This is the stage. You don't have to tell me that, of all people. Our Lord was the first to affirm that all men are equally significant. Your lords and masters, on the other hand'—he pointed to the two photographs on the wall—'are you sure they attach the same significance to the murder of any common pushcart vendor in the Quartieri Spagnoli as they do to Vezzi's murder, for example?"

Ricciardi, surprised by the vehemence of don Pierino's reaction, smiled sadly.

"You're right, Father. You're right. That's not what I meant, but I owe you my apologies in any case. I can see how you might think that, but that's not what I was trying to say. The point is that, day after day, I witness the suffering that people intentionally inflict on other individuals. It's difficult for me to think of love as anything but the prime motive of these crimes. Believe me, Father, if it's not love, it's hunger, in which case it's simpler. Hunger is understandable, one can easily grasp it. It's straightforward, immediate. Love isn't; love takes other paths."

"I can't believe you really think that, Commissario. Love

has nothing to do with this butchery. Love moves the world, it's the love of fathers, of mothers, of God especially. Love is wanting what's good for those you love. Certainly not bloodshed and pain: that's damnation.'

Ricciardi stared at the priest with blazing eyes; he seemed to be nearly shaking from a raging fire within.

"Damnation. Believe me, Father, when I tell you that for you damnation is only a word. Believe me when I tell you that damnation is the relentless perception of sorrow, day in and day out. Other people's sorrow that becomes your own, that stings like a whip, that leaves wounds that won't heal, that go on bleeding, that infect your blood."

The Commissario's voice was now a whisper, his lips barely moving. It was a sharp hiss and don Pierino instinctively leaned back in his chair, somewhat horrified.

"I see it, do you understand, Father? I see it. I feel it, the sorrow of the dead who remain attached to a life they no longer have. I know it; I hear the sound of the blood draining away. The mind that deserts them, the brain clinging by the fingernails to the last shred of life as it runs out. Love, you say? If you only knew how much death there is in your love, Father. How much hate. Man is imperfect, Father, let me tell you. I know it all too well."

Don Pierino stared at the Commissario, wide-eyed. Somehow he understood that Ricciardi was speaking literally, not metaphorically. What was in that man's heart? What were those transparent, desperate eyes concealing? The Assistant Pastor felt an immense compassion, and a human revulsion.

"I . . . I believe in God, Commissario. And I believe that if He gives someone a greater cross to bear than others, He has His reasons. If this someone can help his neighbour more, if he can help a lot of other people, then perhaps his suffering is justified; perhaps it has some meaning, all this sorrow."

Ricciardi slowly regained his composure; he leaned back in

his chair, sighed faintly, closed his eyes and reopened them. Once again he assumed the expressionless face that characterized him. Don Pierino felt relieved, as if for a moment, only a moment, he had had a glimpse of hell.

"You should know, don Pierino, that you have been a great help to me. I promise you that, as we initially agreed, the information you have given me will not be used to send an innocent man to prison. Everything will be verified with the greatest attention."

"I am pleased to have been of help to you, Commissario. I ask one thing in return, however: promise me that you will come and see me, once this dreadful affair is resolved. And that we will go to the opera together. At your expense, of course."

Ricciardi made his usual wry face, which don Pierino had learned to recognize as a smile.

"It's a high price for me, Father. But I can make you that promise."

# XXV

When Maione heard Ricciardi's voice calling him, he could tell from the tone that the investigation had switched gears. Experience had taught him that, with no chance of being mistaken. There was a precise moment during an interrogation, an encounter, a word that led the Commissario to see the truth, find the solution. And at that moment, the predictable exclamation was: 'Maione!' The Brigadier was pleased, for himself and for the Commissario who, once the operation was over, would be able to enjoy a moment of fleeting, illusive peace.

Rubbing his hands, like an old hunting dog that starts wagging his tail when he hears the rifle taken down from the rack, he popped his head in the doorway: 'You called, *Commissa'*?'

Michele Nespoli was twenty-five years old, from Calabria. His family was poor, despite owning a small plot of land and a flock not far from Mormanno, in Sila. Of nine brothers and sisters, he was the third, the first male. From an early age, along with a strong character that was also impulsive and cheerful, he had demonstrated a great passion for singing and had proved to have a beautiful voice. No village feast took place, no gathering of farmers or shepherds, at which Michele was not asked to sing. And when he began to make his angelic voice heard, everyone would smile and stop arguing or even just talking. Neither wine nor playing cards were a sufficient distraction: his voice stopped hearts.

It was therefore natural for the family, and most of the village, to contribute their limited resources to send Michele to study singing at the Conservatory of San Pietro a Majella, in Naples, the largest music school in Southern Italy and among the best in the country.

Growing up, Michele strengthened the timbre of his voice, cultivating a keen intonation and excellent expressivity. Still, as in all areas of life in which one must also earn a living, a little diplomacy and an aptitude for adulation would have been helpful.

Both were completely alien to Michele, however, who on the contrary tended to be quick-tempered and excessively arrogant. He showed this when he reacted to the suggestions of an elderly vocal exercise instructor—a man inclined to give good grades in exchange for cordial behaviour—by slapping him in public. For a few terrible weeks he was suspended from his studies and feared that he had impulsively thwarted years of sacrifices made by him and his fellow villagers. How could he possibly go back to the village? How would he explain it? Fortunately, his indisputable talent salvaged his diploma. But by then he had the reputation of being a quarrelsome, unreliable individual and had a hard time finding engagements to at least support his staying in the city.

It was the start of a period of grim hardship. By day he worked as a waiter in bars, at night he sang on the waterfront or in restaurants, to the accompaniment of drunken clapping. But he was Calabrian and persistent: he would not give up. He had come to Naples as a boy to become a singer and, by God, he would become a singer.

As time passed, however, he began drinking. He told himself ironically that it was to keep up with those who applauded him in the taverns. In actuality he wasn't tired enough at night to fall asleep right away, and the ghost of his failure danced about jubilantly. So to knock himself out he resorted to the cheap wine that he came by, gratis, by singing a little longer than he'd agreed to. He just had to be careful not to overdo it while he was performing, not to affect his diction: otherwise people would laugh at him, something which he detested. He had begun his downfall and would have slipped even deeper, had it not been for what happened on the evening of 20 July 1930.

Ricciardi was very clear about what had to be done now. After the conversation with don Pierino he had realized the true import of the Incident's message, as it regarded Vezzi. Naturally he knew that it was just an inkling, a mere hunch. But it was now apparent to him that the murderer would have had no need to return, once he had escaped through the window, unless he was involved in the performance. Therefore, they had to look at everyone allowed backstage during the opera: singers, extras, stagehands and technicians.

It must have been a man, if he wore Vezzi's overcoat—given the tenor's imposing bulk—and jumped from the window: only four or five feet, granted, but still a good jump. And returned to Vezzi's dressing room at the risk of being spotted, to then go out again without his disguise.

They had to look for something: first of all a pair of shoes with traces of grass from the royal gardens, maybe even a little mud; the crime scene inspection the night of the murder had shown signs of someone landing in the flower bed, marks deep enough to suggest an individual of a certain weight. Perhaps a bloodstained garment or two: given the condition of the dressing room, it didn't seem possible that the murderer could have avoided getting splattered.

Ricciardi got Maione to confirm that the theater had been under guard since the evening of the murder and that, consequently, no one could have carried out any objects or clothing. Then he gave the Brigadier some specific instructions.

"Check the theater's prop room and the wardrobe department, without alarming anyone or putting them on the alert; we need to see if one of the singers, extras or even just a stagehand switched his shoes or clothes. If he did, and wasn't able to dispose of the soiled items somehow, they must still be there. And we have to find them."

"Anyone in particular, *Commissa'*? Who should we be looking at?"

"Males. Males of considerable height and weight."

On 20 July 1930, at eleven o'clock at night, Michele Nespoli was singing *Santa Lucia Luntana* in Trattoria della Mattonella, in the Quartieri Spagnoli. That evening he had started drinking earlier than usual. The summer's fierce heat reminded him, by contrast, of his mountains, the dark, silent Pollino which he sang to from the window of his house in Sila. And of his mother, her rough caresses.

The entire room was charged with the song's poignant melancholy. Everyone there had loved ones who had boarded ships for distant lands, *pe' tterre assaje luntane*, loved ones whom they would never see again. Some leaned their head on the table and wept uncontrollably, though to some extent this was due to the wine that flowed profusely. It was then that a man, whom they later found out had just been released from prison, spoke sharply to Michele, ordering him to sing a different song immediately. Michele, in the middle of the last stanza, his eyes full of emotion, paid no attention and insisted on finishing the song. The man, unsteady on his legs after knocking his chair to the ground, took a knife from the table and shouted again that Michele should stop singing immediately. Looking him squarely in the eye, with a gaze that was both proud and mocking, the singer ended the song with a superb high note; whereupon the man rushed at him, roaring like a beast and brandishing the knife.

There was a brief scuffle; none of those present considered intervening, maybe because their senses were dulled from the food and wine, though more likely to avoid getting in any trouble. The fray lasted all of maybe thirty or forty seconds. When it was over Michele sat on the floor, breathing heavily, his left arm badly slashed. But the man who had attacked him was no longer moving and the knife he had been holding earlier was now sticking out of his chest. Around them a terrible silence had fallen. The owner of the trattoria came up to the singer and said: "*Guaglio'*, you must leave now."

And she opened the door for him. With great effort, Michele went out, staggering, and disappeared into the nocturnal maze of the Quartieri Spagnoli.

The prop room was adjacent to wardrobe, on the fourth floor of the theater. Ricciardi had already seen it, on his earlier visit to Signora Lilla's realm. Managing the props, which included weapons, hats, footwear and so on, was not wardrobe's jurisdiction, however, but that of a spry, spirited old man named Costanzo Campieri. Maione found him at his post and learned that he almost never went home.

"*Brigadie'*, I have no family; all I have is this job. Plus, I'm responsible for the items, and that's no trivial matter. In these times of hunger and desperation, there are people who would kill for a pair of shoes."

"Let's talk about Wednesday night. Was there any unusual activity? Are stage props generally switched?"

Campieri scratched his bald head.

"Sometimes it happens, something can break during the performance and you replace it, if possible, between scenes. Either that or you fix it, if you can. I once repaired the pharaoh's headdress in *Aida* while the singer was still onstage, after it got crushed in back. I'm an artist, that's for sure. Another time . . . "

"Right, you'll tell me about it another time. Let's go back to Wednesday. Did anyone switch something?"

"No, no one came up here. But something strange did happen. I noticed it yesterday, when I made my inspection."

Maione's ears perked up.

"What was it?"

"I found a pair of shoes in place of another. Ordinary shoes, for a man, large, size eleven. Black, standard. Exactly the same as the other pair."

"If they were identical, what made you notice them?

"The fact that I keep the shoes spotless. And the soles of the ones I found had bits of grass and mud on them."

Michele remembered almost nothing from the moment he left the trattoria to when he awoke in an unfamiliar doorway. He vaguely remembered hearing whistles as the police arrived, but he might have imagined it. He had definitely lost a lot of blood and his arm was hurting.

What woke him was the cool feel of a wet handkerchief that had been placed on his forehead and the softness of the cloth that had been propped under his head. He opened his eyes and saw something very strange: a woman studying him up close. A sweet oval face, blue eyes that looked worried and a mouth that was a little pouty; her long hair came to her shoulders and she wore a simple white nightgown. Michele was spellbound, like when the eye is captured by an image that it can't stop seeing.

"Lie still, don't move: you've lost a lot of blood. As soon as you're able to, stand up and come with me. I won't be able to carry you upstairs."

The voice was a whisper, but he could tell the tone was caring and urgent. Making a determined effort, Michele drew himself up into a seated position.

"I can make it now. I'd better go, I don't want to get you in any trouble."

She placed a hand on his uninjured arm to detain him.

"You can't go, it's swarming with cops out there. They're searching up and down, something bad must have happened. I don't want to know about it. Right now though, I told you, you shouldn't even think of moving, otherwise, given the blood you've lost, you could die. Later on, when you recover, if you want to go to the police on your own two feet, it's no business of mine and you can go. But for now, I'm obliged to help you out of Christian charity."

Her argument was convincing, and Michele, moreover, had no desire to go out into the night and meet a doomed fate, when all he'd done was defend himself. And so, leaning on her arm, which was surprisingly strong for such a petite young woman, he let himself be led into the building and up the stairs.

The woman lived alone, in a tiny apartment converted from the attic of the old building. The lavatory they used was on the floor below. In the months Michele remained there, he ran into several people, men and women, who smiled at him without saying a word. He discovered that there was an unspoken solidarity among individuals who live in certain districts, based on *omertà*, an unconditional code of silence toward the outside world. He didn't know what the girl had told them about him, how she had explained his presence or if she had; but in some strange way he felt sure he was safe.

On one of his first days he had overheard a conversation through the open window between two policemen and the caretaker in the courtyard. The cops were asking about him, of course, complete with a description. The woman, whom he had seen more than once, denied knowing him so firmly and positively that he himself, smiling, began to doubt that he was actually there.

Inevitably, as might be expected, he sang. It happened after about a week, while he was shaving his beard at the kitchen sink, with a knife that was sharper than the others. He wasn't even aware of it; it was Saturday and the sun was shining. The girl had gone out to buy some bread and fruit. He was feeling better and felt relaxed. And so he sang, in keeping with his nature. A recent song, quite successful: *Dicitencello Vuje*. At a certain point he realized that the usual sounds of the morning could no longer be heard through the open window. Not even the voices of children playing. He looked out, worried that he had given himself away; maybe the place was being raided by the police.

Instead a small crowd had gathered in the courtyard, three floors below. He saw about a dozen people and some children gazing up, open-mouthed. An elderly woman listened, enthralled. The girl walked into the courtyard, carrying a package wrapped in newspaper, and looked around, confused. The caretaker stepped away from the group, and hugged and kissed her. From a balcony on the second floor, a man in his undershirt even started applauding. To his recollection, Michele had never met with such a vast success. From that day on, for the people of the Quartieri, he had become *'o Cantante*, the Singer, and she *'a 'nnammurata d'o Cantante*, the Singer's sweetheart.

# XXVI

Ricciardi heard Maione's report about the muddy shoes in the San Carlo's prop room with no surprise. He knew that the countdown had already started and that the noose was tightening around the killer. He knew that first the clues, and later the evidence, would both point in the same direction, converging on the incontrovertible truth. As they should do. As they always did.

And so, as usual, he gave Maione the first and last name of the individual on whom to start collecting the information required for the investigation. Maione set off at breakneck speed.

Ricciardi, for his part, headed for the church of San Ferdinando: he was on his way to issue an invitation to don Pierino. He wanted to see the opera that evening.

It was the beginning of autumn when they kissed for the first time. There had been smiles and then caresses, and then that desperate embrace. They had the same rage, the same yearning to overcome hunger, other people, everything. And now they were no longer alone. Since it was clear by now that no one was looking for him anymore, Michele faced the problem of finding a job.

Pride prevented him from being a further burden on his sweetheart's meagre resources; she had a job but her earnings were certainly not handsome. It seemed obvious that he could not go back to singing in trattorias, where they would certainly have heard about what had happened at the Mattonella. So he began making the rounds here and there, among the numerous construction sites in the city, offering his services as a simple labourer. He found a job on the site of the renovation of a building at Monte di Dio, not far from where he lived.

When he went home in the evening, he was exhausted. Physically weakened by the heavy work, he missed the music that had always nourished his soul. And once again, before he fell asleep, the ghosts of the people who had sacrificed so much for him demanded an accounting of what he was doing and, more to the point, what he wasn't doing. But then, in the moonlight shining through the window, he would look at the serene face of his woman and find the justification for everything, and he too would fall asleep.

Still, it was she who was aware of how frustrated Michele was by the situation. One day, when he came home in the rain, she greeted him with a broad smile and told him that, through a friend, she had got him an audition with none other than the orchestra conductor at the San Carlo, Maestro Mariano Pelosi. It was 10 November.

When don Pierino saw Ricciardi standing there, he was concerned. The Commissario had a cold gleam in his eyes, his jaw muscles were twitching and his tightly pressed lips seemed even thinner than usual. His hair, whipped about by the wind, fell over his face, setting off his eyes and making him look even more determined.

"Commissario, so soon! I didn't expect to see you again today. Please, come in. Come and sit down in the sacristy."

"Thank you, Father. I'm sorry to bother you again. But I'm here to keep a recent promise."

"What's that?"

"Will you come with me to the performance this evening? It's important I see it."

Don Pierino assumed a sad expression.

"So, it's work-related, the reason you want to go to the theater. That wasn't what I had in mind when I made you promise that you would go to the opera."

Ricciardi lowered his gaze for a moment. When he looked up at the priest again, his eyes had lost their feverish expression.

"You're right, Father. It is for work and it doesn't absolve me from my promise. I remain obliged to you, and I renew my promise to go and see your favourite opera, at the earliest opportunity. But tonight I'd like to ask you to accompany me just the same, if you're free. I would feel more at ease somehow."

The Assistant Pastor smiled and placed a hand on Ricciardi's arm.

"All right, Commissario. I'll accompany you, as you wish. And I will still help you. I would just like you to be more lenient with yourself, once in a while. And look deep in your heart to find the good feelings that, I know, you feel."

Ricciardi nodded gravely.

"I'll see you tonight, Father. And thanks again."

For Michele it was an enormous thrill to find himself on the stage of the San Carlo. Naturally in his years of study at the Conservatory he had attended numerous operas, gripping the railing of the gallery, holding his breath, and singing the baritone parts in a silent whisper. He was well aware of how suited his voice was to strong roles, those with great emotional impact, and he knew that having kept his vocal cords in shape by singing in taverns would help him perform at the audition in acceptable condition.

With him were a dozen or so candidates. The role being offered was for several operas that would be performed during the season, with a supporting company associated with the theater. The pay was good, but the chance of reviving his dream far exceeded any monetary gains. If he were to get the engagement, the spectre of failure that was constantly with him would finally fade.

He sang with all his heart, with all his soul: *Rigoletto*, his favourite role, came to life with his powerful voice. No one performed with his rage, his passion. Admiration and surprise glowed in Pelosi's eyes, though he had heard many, many singers in his decades-long career. Michele turned out to be the best and got the part.

On the way home, Michele was beside himself with joy. As he embraced his woman, he thought he was on cloud nine.

Since he would have to go to the opera, Ricciardi stopped at home first. He didn't want his *tata* to be unduly worried, fearing her subsequent reaction. This did not spare him a vehement protest however. Rosa pointed out that his failure to keep to a set schedule would cause him stomach problems, and that he had put her on the spot by not warning her in advance, since she had nothing ready for him to eat.

It wasn't true: cold meat and boiled vegetables immediately appeared on the table and Ricciardi thought he ought to go home early every night. To avoid stomach problems.

When he had finished eating, he went to change his clothes, putting on a dark suit. Then he opened the curtains of his bedroom window; even if just for a moment, he didn't want to miss his tacit appointment. He didn't have the slightest idea that Enrica knew he watched her, so her startled surprise as she was setting the table for supper escaped him. He enjoyed the girl's slow, graceful gestures, her charming domestic dance, the facility of her left hand, the femininity of her slightly tilted head as she judged the distance of a plate from the cutlery and the latter from the glasses.

He had to make a great effort to tear himself away from the sight of her. But the encounter he would shortly have summoned him: he couldn't miss the evening at the theater.

*

As arranged, Maione was waiting at the entrance of the Questura. Ricciardi questioned him with his eyes. The Brigadier shook his head.

"There's not much. He lives alone, in an apartment near the Conservatory. But he's only been there a few months, no one knows where he was before. He's studied there a short time, it's his first year, but they say he's good, very good. The rest, tomorrow. I put two men on it: Alinei and Zanini."

"All right. Keep me updated, moment to moment. Now let's go. Don Pierino must already be waiting out there."

The San Carlo had resumed its usual appearance: there was less elegance and sophistication compared to opening night, but more genuine passion and knowledge in the audience. As he waited for Ricciardi, Don Pierino observed the faces of the spectators who gradually converged on the theater's main entrance; he amused himself by trying to predict which row number each of them would be seated in, based on their clothes, their age and the expression on their faces. He liked the theater more, on those evenings. He could sense the love for opera, the familiarity with the scores, and it didn't even bother him if loud whistling sometimes chastised a mistake made by one of the singers, though he himself was more indulgent. How could you be critical of those who were trying to give you such a beautiful gift, such feeling?

When the Commissario arrived, accompanied by Brigadier Maione, the priest went to meet him, in high spirits.

"My dear Commissario, good evening! Even if you're here for work, you won't fail to be enchanted by the theater's atmosphere!"

Ricciardi, casting a quick glance around, took him by the arm.

"Quiet, Father! Tonight there is no Commissario and no work. No one must know I'm here. Show me the way you usually get in."

Confused, don Pierino apologized with a look and indicated the end of the portico, where a recessed niche hid the small door of the side entrance. The three men walked in that direction and went in. Patrisso, the caretaker, came towards them, not recognizing them at first.

"I'm sorry, gentlemen, this is a service entrance, you can't . . . oh, don Pierino, is it you? And . . . Brigadier, Commissario, good evening! How can I help you?"

It was Maione who spoke up.

"Good evening, Patrisso. Why is the door is still open on this side?"

"This entrance is for stage personnel and materials and such that are brought in up until a quarter of an hour before the performance starts. Then we close up on this side. If someone has to go out, there's the little door in the lobby that leads to the royal gardens. In an emergency, let's say. I was just about to lock up now."

Ricciardi wondered if the entry of a murderer could be considered an emergency. Yes or no, that's what the little door to the gardens had been used for on the night of the opening.

"Listen, Patrisso, does it ever happen that someone, one of the singers maybe, might enter or leave during the performance?"

Patrisso shrugged.

"*Commissa'*, how should I know? I told you, we lock up and we go to support the staff at the main entrance. Of course, I think some may go out to smoke. They can't smoke backstage because it's dangerous. You wouldn't believe how much these singers smoke. And they make their living on their voice. Or else they may go out to get a breath of air, or stretch their legs. Not with this wind, though. A chill is a singer's worst enemy."

The three men listened attentively. Ricciardi was mentally reconstructing the possible events on opening night; by now he was confident he knew how things had gone and even who the murderer might be, at least allowing for a certain margin for error. Any additional information would be able to confirm his theory. This did not mean that the Commissario was satisfied, only that he was getting closer to the truth.

He thought about Vezzi's image that still haunted the locked dressing room: knees slightly bent, hand outstretched, the desperate song of an aria that wasn't his. And the tears, the tears streaming down his painted face. An immense, ultimate sorrow, that did not allow for pardon. He was the executor of an extreme vengeance, his own doom. With Maione and don Pierino, Ricciardi headed for the narrow staircase leading to the area backstage and the dressing rooms. He was thinking about death.

## XXVII

Michele Nespoli was ready, even though he would not make his entrance until later: the prelude, the chorus, the sopranos' duet, then him. He wasn't thinking about the opera. He was thinking about death.

He sensed that they would once again prevent him from singing. That was the thing that weighed most heavily on him. And this time he wouldn't even have the solace of that face sleeping beside him, that he could gaze at in the moonlight. Not that he was sorry, no. He had done what he had to do. He had acted, once again, in accordance with his code of honour. With what he had learned from the stories of old men sitting around the fire, during those terrible winter nights in Sila, with the howling of wolves outside the door and the barking of terrified dogs. A code imprinted in his nature, that always made him clash, however, and set him at odds with the world of men. With this city, where the strong were permitted to take advantage of the weak.

Michele Nespoli was a man who loved and this was a sin for which they never forgave him. He loved music, he loved singing. And he loved a woman, whose smile had made him want to go on living.

When he took the engagement he had had to find a place of his own: the intolerant theater management did not approve of cohabitation without marriage; they might throw him out. He had waited until Christmas Day to ask her to marry him. He was looking forward to her surprised, joyful face, the toss of her blonde hair, her embrace. Instead, her face had turned sad, her smile sorrowful. No, she replied: not yet, at least. There were some things she had to resolve, they would talk about it. He had to trust her, wait and be patient.

Michele remembered his acute surprise, the anguish he had felt, anger, too, and the first violent stab of jealousy. But he had no alternative: he loved her, the only way he knew how to love, utterly and completely. He would wait. Meanwhile, it was enough to see her, even from afar.

The blonde woman was listening to the music. At first she'd thought she wouldn't go, just to be safe. But then, on second thought, she decided to be there: it would have raised too many questions otherwise, too much talk.

She had to avoid that, absolutely. Avoid having prying eyes aimed at her and her man, having people talk, make insinuations. She had to be there to keep an eye on things, to get some indication, to forestall.

Her senses alert, her eyes vigilant, she followed the performance with extreme attention. She knew every note, every scene. She knew what positions the singers would take, which pieces the orchestra would play. She greeted the friends she met, betraying no emotion, not making a move that was unusual.

She smiled at her man, meeting his eyes, to reassure him: she was there, and she would always be there.

Don Pierino didn't get it: even if they were there unofficially, why not sit in the audience? Or, perhaps, in one of the side balconies, from which they would have had a better view of the stage?

Instead, the Commissario had led him almost on to the stage, between the rigging and hoists that were used to change the sets. The Brigadier, at a sign from Ricciardi, had then left them and gone back down to the secondary entrance. Don

Pierino sighed, resigned: would he ever be able to enjoy an opera seated comfortably in the audience?

Ricciardi stepped closer to him.

"Who's coming onstage now?"

"No one, Commissario. First there's just music, very soft. Then Turiddu sings. A serenade, to Lola."

"Alfio's wife, right?"

"Yes, Alfio's wife."

After a brief prelude, with the curtain lowered, a beautiful male voice began to sing. Don Pierino noticed that Ricciardi was continually checking his watch, noting the times in pencil on a piece of paper.

"What is he saying, Father? I can't understand him."

"It's a serenade in Sicilian dialect, Commissario. He's telling her how beautiful she is and that her beauty is worth damnation; he also tells her, but it's only poetry, you understand, that he would be willing to be killed for her and that if she isn't in heaven, it's not worth going there. It's prophetic, because in the end he is killed by Alfio."

The two spoke in a whisper. At the end of the song, as the orchestra went on playing alone, the curtain rose. After a purely musical interlude, men and women entered, and after taking their places on the stage, began to engage in a choral dialogue. Ricciardi relaxed and don Pierino hoped he was enjoying the beauty of the music. Unfortunately, however, he sensed that the Commissario's thoughts were elsewhere.

Maione returned, his bulky overcoat covering his uniform. He was breathing somewhat heavily, as if his hefty body had been subjected to some unusual exertion. Don Pierino noticed that the Brigadier's shoes bore traces of fresh mud, along with a few blades of grass. Had he gone out? And where to?

The Brigadier spoke to Ricciardi.

"All done, *Commissa'*."

"All right then, let's check: did you leave when I told you?"

The Brigadier checked his wristwatch, holding it a distance away, being far-sighted.

"Yes, I think so. My watch read seven minutes past eight. From the stage to the dressing room, less than a minute. From the window to the dressing room, two minutes, including the time it took to open the door of the gardens, which I wasn't familiar with. But it's easy, a normal lock. From the dressing room to the stage, another minute, even less."

Ricciardi was keeping count on the tips of his nervous fingers.

"Barely four minutes to account for the movements. Let's see, then."

He turned to don Pierino.

"Father, what happens when a singer leaves the stage and then has to return to it?"

"Well, it depends. If he has to return immediately or almost, he waits in the wings. If instead he has a longer interval, then he goes back to his dressing room: retouches his make-up, straightens his clothes. He doesn't go outdoors, partly to avoid draughts which are always possible when going from one temperature to another."

The little priest continued to whisper, waving his hands in his characteristic way.

"But is the way to the dressing rooms from the stage the same for everyone?" Ricciardi asked.

"Yes. First come the dressing rooms of the orchestra conductor and the principal singers, then the common ones for the other singers and the extras in costume."

Ricciardi's crystalline green eyes gleamed in the darkness, as onstage Santuzza and Lucia sang their duet. Behind the Commissario, Maione's imposing figure kept watch in the shadows.

"And tell me, Father, to get to the common dressing rooms, you have to pass those of the principals? Are you sure?"

"Yes, Commissario. I just told you."

On the stage, the women's duet over, a new character had entered, dressed as a rustic villager, and singing in a deep voice. A tall young man with broad shoulders. Ricciardi glanced quickly at Maione, who nodded his head slowly. The Commissario again turned to the priest, tilting his head toward the singer.

"And him?"

"That's compare Alfio, the baritone who later on sings the lines you quoted this morning. He's Lola's husband, the one who kills compare Turiddu at the end."

"And the singer? Who is he? Do you know him?"

"Yes, I've heard him a few times this season. He's a very talented young man, if you ask me. He has a career ahead of him. Nespoli is his name. Michele Nespoli."

Onstage, Michele, seated at a table with a glass in his hand, thundered: "*M'aspetta a casa Lola, che m'ama e mi consola, ch'è tutta fedeltà.*" Lola awaits me at home, the woman who loves and consoles me and is wholly faithful to me.

The opera continued; the company performed well together, the singers perfectly suited to their respective characters. The audience, Ricciardi thought, seemed to be enjoying it quite a bit, and on several occasions there was spontaneous, heartfelt applause. In addition to his voice, Nespoli was notable for his stage presence. His athletic, imposing build helped him stand out, and he sang with the passion and enthusiasm of a man who lives and breathes just to sing. The Commissario, hands in his pockets, took it all in with a watchful eye, not missing a word.

He moved only when, at the end of a dramatic duet with Santuzza, he heard the lines that he had come to know: "*Io sangue voglio, all'ira m'abbandono, in odio tutto l'amor mio finì . . .* " I will have vengeance . . . , all my love shall end in hate. Repeated several times, with force and rage, by Nespoli. To Ricciardi they seemed very different from when he had heard them from Vezzi's dead lips, more than one might reasonably expect.

The tenor, in his high, modulated voice, was expressing regret over what happened: Vezzi's image meant to convey, Ricciardi finally understood now, the emotion that had guided the killer's hand. The second singer, with the deep timbre of his baritone voice and his eyes flashing with rage, was articulating his own feelings. The Commissario had no doubt that Nespoli, after two days, still felt the full reverberation of his vengeance. In fact, he wondered how the audience, the other singers, even don Pierino, who, as usual, was murmuring the lines to himself, hadn't noticed it and been horrified.

With a final, terrible "I will have vengeance!" Nespoli ran offstage, unknowingly passing right under the noses of the three hidden spectators. The audience got to its feet in a furious round of applause that drowned out the music of the orchestra. From his position Ricciardi, who glanced quickly at his watch just as Maione had done, saw the expression in the singer's eyes: they were vacant, as though he were thinking of something else.

The baritone did not pause to hear the applause, which gave no sign of stopping; hastily he descended the stairs that separated him from the dressing rooms and Ricciardi. The Commissario took a few steps after him, and saw that he passed Vezzi's door without looking at it, his head held high and his gaze focused straight ahead. Ricciardi looked at his watch again and went back to his place, as the orchestra started playing again.

When Nespoli came back onstage, with a ringing *"A voi tutti salute!"*—good health to you all!—exactly nine minutes and fifty-six seconds had passed. Ricciardi thought it was more than enough time. He was a grim, silent observer of the story's ending and of the roaring success the opera enjoyed that evening as well. Don Pierino and Maione watched him, the one oblivious and the other well aware of the thoughts that were going through the Commissario's head. The difference between Nespoli's expression and that of the other members of the company when they were individually called back to the stage to receive the public's ovation did not escape any of them: the baritone smiled with his mouth, but not with his eyes. Ricciardi looked at Alfio's shoes and the faint marks left by Maione's shoes on the floor he had walked across. Mud and a bit of grass. The picture was complete.

Ricciardi said goodnight to don Pierino while the public, on its feet, was still applauding.

"Thank you, Father. Once again, thank you very much. Your help has been vital. Now it's time for the hard part of my job, and I have to do it on my own. My promise still stands; I'll come and see you."

The Assistant Pastor looked at him steadily, his lively, spirited dark eyes staring into the other's unwavering, expressionless green gaze.

"Goodnight, Commissario. May God help you make the right choice, for others will pay for your mistakes. If you need me, for my services, you will find me available. Day or night."

With one last intense look, Ricciardi turned and walked towards the dressing rooms, followed by Maione.

## XXVIII

As he walked off the stage, Michele Nespoli knew instantly that it was all over. As soon as he saw the two men standing there motionless, their hands in their pockets, in front of the door, *that* door, he knew right away.

He was surprised to feel relieved, more so than he would have imagined; he couldn't live with that constant threat over his head. Maione stepped forwards and touched his arm.

"Are you Michele Nespoli? We have to ask you a few questions. Please, come inside," he pointed to Vezzi's dressing room, the door to which had been repaired.

A stunned silence fell around them. The still heavy breathing of those who had just left the set was palpable; those who were near the baritone instinctively moved away and left him alone in the middle of a small imaginary stage.

The three men entered the dressing room. Inside, everything had been cleaned up. There was no trace of the tenor's blood anymore, except for some damp stains on the carpet. The mirror had been replaced. If it weren't for Vezzi's image, which he could still see in the corner of the room, though it was fading by now, Ricciardi would have had a hard time recognizing the crime scene that had appeared to him only two days before. Nespoli, who had not lowered his eyes for a moment, looked around briefly, his intense dark gaze pausing at the window, which like before was open partway.

Maione had finished stating Nespoli's name and referencing the occasion of the murder, and silence now fell in the dressing room. Ricciardi stared fixedly at the baritone, who met his gaze boldly. It was the Commissario who spoke.

"Who is the woman?"

Nespoli sighed, slowly.

"I don't know what you're talking about."

Ricciardi nodded his head faintly, as if he had somehow expected that reply.

It was Maione, without altering his tone, who stepped in.

"Would you tell us about what happened the night of March the twenty-fifth, the day before yesterday?"

Nespoli exhaled sharply, irritated.

"What do you think happened?"

Ricciardi took a couple of steps and turned again to the baritone, his back to the corner where Vezzi's image continued spewing out blood.

"We have reason to believe that, for undetermined reasons, you intentionally or unintentionally killed Arnaldo Vezzi; that you killed him on the night of March the twenty-fifth, between seven and nine P.M."

Nespoli smiled, again only stretching his lips. His eyes were those of a caged animal.

"And on what basis do you have reason to believe such a thing?"

They went on staring at one another. Maione stayed where he was, centred between the two of them. Outside the door a constant murmuring could be heard.

The Brigadier said calmly: "We're the ones asking the questions."

The singer did not seem particularly shaken by the accusation.

"Then ask," he said disdainfully.

"Did you encounter Vezzi on the day and time of the crime?"

"I saw him, yes. I ran into him."

"Where?"

Nespoli gave a faint sigh, looking around briefly.

"Right here. Or rather, out there; at the door, I mean."

"At the door?"

"Yes, at the door. I was coming from the stage, on my way back to the dressing room."

"And you spoke to him?"

"He spoke to me."

Until that moment, Ricciardi had not intervened in the conversation; he had been staring at Nespoli the entire time, studying his behaviour. Now he spoke, in a low voice.

"Look, Nespoli, you're in a difficult position. We have our facts and the evidence we need: not being forthcoming will make us waste a little more time, but it will certainly not save you. It will be better for you if you stop pretending you don't understand what we're asking you."

Nespoli turned to the Commissario and smiled.

"If you have this evidence, why are you wasting all this time?"

"Because we have to reconstruct everything that's happened, that's why. And because," here Ricciardi lowered his voice even further, "we have to know if there were accomplices."

A silence fell. Nespoli and Ricciardi stared at one another. Maione glanced from one to the other, his eyelids half-closed as if he were about to fall asleep: his way of staying focused.

Finally Nespoli said: "Evidence, you say? What evidence could you have?" Restrained like that, his powerful voice sounded like distant thunder.

"We found the shoes you switched so as not to track mud from the gardens on to the stage. You're the only one who had prop room shoes of that size checked out to you at that time. You have big feet. You're among the limited number of people who had access to the dressing rooms, the only one who could wear Vezzi's clothes. And lastly, you were seen re-entering from the stairs and you were recognized."

Maione gave no sign of being surprised by the small trap that Ricciardi had set for the baritone: they both knew that it was only circumstantial evidence and that don Pierino could never be sure that the individual he had met on the stairs was Nespoli rather than Vezzi or anyone else of that size. But the Brigadier knew that at times their work resembled mullet fishing, which he did on Sundays near the port; and the mullet, this time too, took the bait.

Nespoli swallowed it with a sigh and a smile, shaking his head slightly. "The priest. Damn it."

He seemed more amused than dejected, as if he had lost a hand at a card game. Ricciardi, his voice still low, said: "What did you have against Vezzi? What had he done to you?"

"He was a bastard. A vile, despicable man. He seduced women. He took liberties with them. He thought he was God. And he wasn't God, he was a zero."

"And so you killed him."

"I certainly didn't intend to kill him. We argued, got into a fight. I punched him, and he ended up in the mirror. Tall as me, heavier than me, yet as soon as I laid a finger on him he ended up in the mirror. Even in that respect, he was worthless."

Silence. Ricciardi turned and saw the tears streaming down the clown's face. He looked at Nespoli again.

"So he didn't deserve to live, Nespoli? And you thought you were God and you came here to kill him."

The baritone gave a start.

"No, I'm not God. But as far as I'm concerned, good is good, and bad is bad. And Vezzi was bad. He didn't even make an attempt to appear good. With that poor Pelosi, for instance, at the rehearsal. I had gone to watch, you can't imagine how he treated him. Pelosi is a good man; he drinks, but he's a decent person who never harms anyone. Vezzi called him an incompetent old drunk, that's what he called him. Heartless."

"And women? You mentioned women."

"Yes, women. He got too familiar with them, he was free with his hands, he demanded their attentions by force, owing to the power he had, because he was important, because he was the famous Vezzi. And now he's nothing."

Nespoli spoke calmly, in a normal, conversational tone. There was no sign of emotion in his voice. But his eyes—his eyes flashed with a savage fury. Ricciardi thought curiously that he would have made a magnificent movie actor, not the new talkies, but the silent films: his expressions wouldn't require captions, the music would be enough.

"Tell us how it happened, exactly."

Nespoli shrugged briefly.

"What can I tell you? I was going back to the dressing room, I had finished my first scene, I had about ten minutes. He had his door open, he looked at me and made a sarcastic comment: 'The amateur, bravo! You sounded like a singer, almost!' I saw red. I gave him a shove, he fell backwards. He got up and said to me: 'You're finished. After this you'll never sing again.' I stepped inside, I closed the door behind me. I tried to apologize, but he repeated: 'After this you'll never sing again.' So I stopped thinking and I punched him."

"How did you punch him? Where?"

Nespoli simulated a right hook.

"Like this. In the face. I caught him under the eye, I think."

It corresponded to the blow's mark on the body.

"And then?"

"Then he fell back into the mirror and it shattered. He started bleeding from his throat, in spurts, a ton of blood. He was wheezing, he sat down in the chair, the blood kept gushing out. The bastard, he was the one who was done singing. With that insincere voice he used to make fun of everybody. With that black soul of his."

Ricciardi, out of the corner of his eye, glanced at the black soul who, weeping, was still singing and gushing blood. Still, he had a right to live, he thought. No matter how black his soul was.

"And what did you do?"

"I thought quickly. I couldn't leave through the dressing-room door, someone might see me. But if I went out through the window and then came back in during the performance, dressed in costume, it would have seemed odd. In effect, it would be like confessing. So I took the bastard's coat, hat and scarf from the armoire and climbed down from the window."

He pointed with his chin to where he had gone out.

"And what door did you come back in from?"

"The little door, near the entrance to the gardens. It's always open; we go out there to smoke during rehearsals."

"And did you meet anyone, coming back?"

"Only the priest; he was towards the top of the stairs. But he was engrossed, he was listening to the intermezzo. I didn't think he had recognized me. I still had a little time, I thought."

"What did you do then? Did you go back to your dressing room?"

"No. How could I? Wearing Vezzi's coat and hat? Besides, even if after the intermezzo there's the chorus and almost everyone is onstage, there's always someone in the dressing room. I looked around carefully, and when I saw that there was no one about, I opened the door and tossed the coat, hat and scarf into the room with Vezzi. They were still playing the end of the intermezzo."

Ricciardi looked at Maione, who nodded. The timing corresponded to what had been clocked that evening.

"Then I locked the dressing-room door and took the utility lift up to the prop room to switch the shoes."

"And the key?"

Nespoli appeared disoriented for a moment.

"The key? I put it in my pocket and later, when I left, I went to the port and threw it in the sea."

Ricciardi stared at him, eye to eye. Nespoli held his gaze.

"How did you explain the fact that the shoes were muddy to the prop manager?"

"Campieri? He wasn't at his post, maybe he had been called away elsewhere or had wandered off somewhere. If he had been there, I would have wiped them off as best I could and gone onstage, running the risk of leaving traces. At that point I had no choice. In any case, there was no more time, I had to go back onstage."

There was a moment's silence. The murmuring outside the door was a backdrop to the long look exchanged between the singer and the detective. Maione was breathing heavily. Vezzi's soul wept and sang and demanded justice, but only Ricciardi heard it.

Nespoli said: "I'm not sorry. I'll never be sorry."

Ricciardi went out first, while Maione fastened the cuffs on Nespoli's wrists. The crowd that had gathered outside the dressing room suddenly fell silent. The theater director made his way through, accompanied by the stage manager: the little Duke was so agitated that he appeared cyanotic.

"This is too much, far, far too much! To come in through the side door during the performance, sneak on to the stage, even! And then into a dressing room! Will you get it through your heads, once and for all, that this is a theater? One of the nation's greatest?"

While the Duke pirouetted around, unable to pause even to catch his breath, Ricciardi noticed that the murmuring of the assorted crowd of clowns, colombinas, harlequins and wagoners had again gone silent. Turning towards the dressing room, he saw Nespoli come out, followed by Maione. The man's gaze remained proud, confident and challenging; the people closest to him stepped back, instinctively. Nespoli looked around, just once: and that was when it happened.

The Commissario noticed that for an instant, one brief, single moment, Nespoli's eyes changed. It was so sudden and fleeting that he doubted whether he had actually seen it; but accustomed as he was to gauging people's emotions from their eyes, he couldn't have been mistaken.

In that one instant, Nespoli's face had become tender and sad, submissive and despairing. The strong, scornful baritone was gone, giving way to a forlorn young man who was nonetheless willing to give up his own life for love. It was an expression of extreme sacrifice.

Ricciardi recalled that, some years before, he had dealt with the murder of a woman by her husband, whom she had wanted to leave for a lover: the man had killed himself, after killing her, with two shots of his army officer's pistol. The Commissario could still recall the murderer's image: half his skull had been blown away by the shot. The one remaining eye, however, had precisely the same expression as it shed desperate tears. Giving one's life for love. The image kept saying, "*For you, my love, for you*," while the brain still sizzled from the heat of the gunpowder.

Ricciardi immediately looked around at the crowd, to figure out who the singer had searched out with his eyes. He knew that the key to it all was there, in that look: the real motive for Vezzi's murder, and Nespoli's own perdition. He glanced around and, at first, as the theater director went on sputtering and protesting, he could see no possible recipient of such a look. Then, unexpectedly, he recognized the mirror image of the baritone's eyes. While the singer's eyes were submissive, adoring and quivering with sacrifice, their counterpart was almost menacing: be careful not to give yourself away, they said, make sure you keep up that pose.

The moment passed, leaving the Commissario confused. This new element, which he did not intend to underestimate, once again changed the perspective and radically so. And yet they had a confession, a full confession, which he couldn't overlook.

Nespoli's appearance had had the incidental, though not negligible, effect of silencing the theater director for a moment. But only for a moment.

"But . . . but . . . is this what it seems? Have you arrested the guilty party? Oh, but then I must take it all back! My congratulations! Not that I ever for a moment doubted that justice would triumph, nevertheless this last . . . raid of yours would have led me to take matters up with your superiors again or, if necessary, with Rome, to resolve the issue. But now, of course, if it should turn out that you really found your man . . . "

Ricciardi, his voice loud enough to be heard throughout the area said: "Yes, Duke. That's exactly right. We have arrested the perpetrator, so it would seem."

Everyone had something to say about Ricciardi's announcement and for a moment there was a babel of confused voices. Only one person, whom the Commissario was watching, did not raise her eyes.

## XXIX

When he caught up with Maione outside the theater, they headed for the Questura. The procedure was irregular, because for safety reasons they should have been accompanied by at least two policemen. However, the man under arrest had such a quiet, submissive attitude that there seemed no danger of being shot in the head. A few hundred yards further on, they ran into Luise, the young reporter from *Il Mattino*, who was out of breath.

"Commissario, hello . . . I was notified by phone . . . who is the man you've arrested? Can you tell me, this time?"

Ricciardi took pity on the young man whom he had treated badly at their first meeting, and didn't want to send him away empty-handed.

"It's one of the singers from *Cavalleria Rusticana*, his name is Michele Nespoli. He's a suspect."

Nespoli, who had kept his eyes lowered until then, looked up and said scornfully: "What hotshots these cops are! They always catch the offender. Especially when they have an informer."

Maione placed a hand on his shoulder.

"Speak only when you're questioned."

Luise tried to ask something about the circumstances of the arrest, but the three men quickly walked away.

Once the detainment procedures were completed and Nespoli had been taken to a holding cell in the Questura, Ricciardi said goodnight to Maione.

"Don't arrange for the transfer to Poggioreale yet. Tomorrow I want to talk to him one more time."

"Something isn't clear to you, huh, *Commissa'*? I realized it from the questions you asked and by the way you looked at him. Still, he confessed."

"Yes, he confessed. But tomorrow I want to talk to him again. Goodnight."

On his way back home, the Commissario went over the sequence of events.

The look, first of all: with handcuffs on his wrists, Nespoli had looked at a person whom Ricciardi would never have expected. The randomness of the act: was it possible for an individual—even one with a disposition as quick-tempered as that of the baritone—to react in such an extreme way, over a simple comment? The timing: was it possible for someone singing in an opera to leave the stage, kill a man, escape through a window, come back in, go up to the fourth floor, switch his shoes, come back down and go onstage to sing—all in just ten minutes, without having planned it? The method: was it possible for a single punch—which moreover had raised the doctor's doubts about its limited effects—to knock a person down so violently as to shatter a heavy mirror and cause him to bleed to death? Possible, of course; he had seen even stranger circumstances. But unlikely, very unlikely. Finally, the Incident: the tears streaming down Vezzi's face. You don't cry during a fight over such senseless reasons.

So then, Ricciardi thought, Nespoli was covering for someone. But who? And why? The woman he had looked at? Was she perhaps cognizant of events, or even an accomplice? And how could he get to the truth, at this point? Did Nespoli have a clear idea of what he was letting himself in for? Besides his career, irreparably ruined, the singer would lose his freedom for many, many years. Even if it wasn't intentional, Vezzi's murder was heinous and had become a focal point for the press and for the powers in Rome. The judges, Ricciardi was well aware, were always eager to please the regime, and the tenor had been their favourite darling. The Commissario was willing to bet that the sentence would be exemplary.

It was around eleven o'clock by the time he got home. His *tata* Rosa, her conscience silenced by the evening snack she had left him, had gone to bed, as evidenced by the deep snoring coming from her room. Ricciardi retired to his room and changed out of his clothes. Just to be sure, he went to the window, opened the curtains, and looked at the window across from him.

Enrica sat sewing by the tenuous light of the lamp. Having set aside her trousseau, she wanted to finish a summer garment for her little nephew who would soon be one year old. It was to be her birthday gift to him. She loved her sister's son very much, and she often wondered if she would love a son of her own that much, or even more, if she were ever to have one. She sighed and instinctively glanced outside. When she saw that the curtains of the window across the way were open at such an odd hour, she started imperceptibly.

Examining the embroidery she had completed on the front of the garment she smiled to herself, thinking that her parents were right: ever since she was a child they had been telling her that she was pig-headed. She reached out for the scissors, there on the table.

Across the windswept street, in the darkness of his room, Ricciardi watched Enrica sew. As always, he imagined that sooner or later he would talk to her and tell her how seeing her embroider made him feel at peace. He would ask her to embroider for him and she would smile, tilt her head to the side and say yes, in that voice that he had never heard; and he would sit there and watch her.

Meanwhile, across the way, her work was done. Enrica put down her embroidery, lifted the scissors from the table with her right hand, passed them to her left and snipped the end of the thread.

And Ricciardi saw it all clearly.

The ribbon with the scissors, which were missing; someone who worked with her left hand; the significance of what the doctor had said two days before; the smock that was too big. And, most importantly, he understood that look that had lasted just a moment.

He also thought, looking across the street, that a momentary look can mean a great deal: it can mean everything.

He had just hung up his coat in the office, when Vice Questore Garzo rushed in like a fury; behind him, extremely agitated, came Ponte, his clerk.

"Ricciardi, is what I heard this morning true? That you've arrested a suspect in the Vezzi homicide? Is it true?"

Ricciardi closed the armoire door, sighed and turned to his superior.

"Yes, it's true. Last night."

Garzo was beside himself: red blotches had appeared on his usually smiling, composed face, his tie was loosened and his hair looked rumpled.

"And why wasn't I notified? I told you clearly, more than once, that any developments, no matter how minimal, were to be reported to me at once. And you arrest the perpetrator without informing me? If it weren't for my friend, the managing editor at *Il Mattino*, who phoned me this morning to congratulate me, I wouldn't have known anything about it! Who am I? Nobody?"

Ricciardi looked at him coldly, his hands in his pockets.

'You are in my office shouting and I don't think that's the proper way to ask me for information. I couldn't have informed you yesterday, because it was eleven o'clock at night and you had been gone for over two hours. What's more, the man is a suspect, not a perpetrator. I communicate with you the way I should communicate, that is through official channels. What your friends tell you doesn't interest me."

He had spoken softly, almost in a whisper, and the contrast with Garzo's yelling was enormous. Just outside the door, Ponte lowered his head as if he had taken a punch. Maione, who had come running, smiled broadly, covering his grin with one hand while holding the newspaper in the other.

Garzo stood there as if embalmed. He blinked two or three times and finally took a deep breath. He looked around and seemed surprised to find himself in Ricciardi's office. When he spoke again, his tone seemed subdued, but there was a fierce quaver in his voice.

"Of course . . . of course. I apologize. Forgive me, Ricciardi. Well then . . . can you kindly tell me something about the arrest you made yesterday so I can report to the Questore? You know, so he won't find himself unprepared when they call from Rome."

He was almost spelling it out, containing his anger. Ricciardi even felt some pity for him.

"Yes, of course. So then: certain elements that emerged from the investigation made us focus our suspicions on Michele Nespoli, a professional singer, a baritone, at the Royal Theater of San Carlo. When interrogated at the scene by myself and Brigadier Maione, to whom most of the credit for the arrest is due, he confessed to the crime. But several other elements must be verified in order to consider the theory of potential accomplices or motives not currently known to us. For this reason, I would not issue any official statements at the present time."

Garzo opened and closed his mouth: what popped into Ricciardi's mind was an image of a big codfish in a suit and tie. When he was able to speak again, he said: "I'm not sure I understand. Didn't you tell me that this Nespoli confessed to killing Vezzi?"

"Yes, but—"

Garzo held up a hand.

"No! No buts! If we have a confession, and we have one, I don't see any reason for uncertainty. I ask you to understand, once and for all: it's one thing to discover the killer two days after the murder, another thing to go on investigating after a confession. If you continue investigating despite having a confession in hand, it means that the solution came out of the blue without us uncovering it and, therefore, there's no merit to solving the case. Now, I believe I am expressing the Questore's opinion by decidedly choosing the first theory, that Nespoli acted alone. And so, my dear Ricciardi, on the one hand,"—and here he indicated the number one by gripping the thumb of his left hand with the index finger and thumb of his right—"I offer you my most heartfelt congratulations for your brilliant work in solving the case; on the other,"—and with the same fingers he grasped his left index finger—"I urge you to refrain from continuing the investigation as well as from communicating any of your concerns to anyone. Do we agree?"

Ricciardi hadn't moved a muscle.

"No. I don't agree by any means. There's the risk of letting one or more guilty parties go free, and you know it. Not to mention remaining in the dark about various aspects of this case that cannot currently be explained."

There was a moment's silence. Maione and Ponte, in the doorway, looked like two statues. Garzo roused himself.

"I have no intention of reconsidering the matter, Ricciardi. That was an order. And another thing: we both know how many times you came and intervened with me, to support the positions of your closest co-workers, and how much you care about them. I would therefore remind you that any disobedience will be attributed not just to you, but also to them. So that Brigadier Maione here, for example, would go from a commendation and a more than likely cash bonus to a severe disciplinary action. Be advised."

At that he turned and walked out with military bearing. Ponte stepped aside to let him pass and followed after him, feigning a look of distress. Maione entered Ricciardi's office, his face flushed. "What a shitty bastard he is!" he said as he closed the door behind him.

## XXX

Ricciardi slumped into the chair behind the desk. He looked glumly at Maione sitting in front of him.

"You hear that? So, either you're a hero or you too are a criminal. No middle ground."

Maione looked at him in silence. Ricciardi sighed.

"I have to take you off the case, Brigadier. From this point on, you will no longer be involved with the investigation. You deserve a nice bonus for the work you've done."

Maione went on looking at him.

"So, Maione. You can go."

"*Commissa'*, I'm not going anywhere. Aside from the fact that I don't take orders from that guy," he nodded toward the door, "but from my immediate supervisor, namely you, I know you by now: and I know when a job is finished and when it isn't. And as I see it, we haven't finished here yet. I realized it last night already and I was sure of it this morning when I saw your face. Besides, the urge to prove to that man and his little dog Ponte that he's wrong is too strong for me to resist. Plus, I really don't give a damn about the bonus: my kids aren't used to having a lot of money. Those kids with too much money turn out bad. Finally," he concluded, mimicking the Vice Questore and holding the tip of his left pinkie with two fingers of his right hand, "only one thing bothers me more than seeing a guilty party go free: seeing an innocent man go to prison."

Ricciardi shook his head and sighed again.

"I knew you were a stubborn old man. One of these days

remind me that I should make you retire. You're right though: we haven't finished here yet. There are some things that aren't clear to me, that must be brought to light, then we can rest.'

Maione put the newspaper on the desk.

"As far as the paper is concerned, we're already heroes. Listen to this: 'The police, after only two days of tireless investigation, discover and bring to justice the brutal murderer of the tenor Vezzi. See the news section for details.' If we're tireless, we must continue slogging away. That's what the word means, doesn't it?"

"Right. However, we have to be wary of Garzo and his people, so here's what we'll do: you take a nice one-day leave, which I'll approve, ostensibly to take your child to the doctor. Instead, see what you can do. Are you still in touch with that guy who lives above the Quartieri, what was his name . . . Bambinella? The one who has a finger in every pie, who knows everybody's business."

"The transvestite? Sure I am. Whenever we pick up a few hookers, that guy is always among them, dressed as a woman and, forgive me *Commissa'*, but he looks better than the real ones. He's *simpatico* though, a million laughs."

"That's the one. Track him down right away, this morning. And ask him about this name."

Ricciardi took a sheet of paper, and after dipping his pen in the inkwell, wrote a name and handed the note to the Brigadier.

"Everything you can find out. *Everything*. Then come to me and report."

Maione read the name, nodded and smiled.

"So she's the one, huh? I noticed that he looked at her strangely. I was sure you hadn't missed it either. Okay, *Commissa'*. Don't give it another thought."

"One last thing, then you can go. Have them bring in Nespoli."

*

It was obvious that Nespoli hadn't slept a wink. He appeared with deep shadows under his eyes and dark stubble on his face, his thick head of hair in disarray. The spectre of his life's failure had begun to dance around him again and this time, he knew, it would never stop. In the cell, his father and mother, siblings and fellow villagers had passed before his mind's eye: all those who had given up a little or a lot to enable him to study, for the joy of seeing him sing at the San Carlo. And now that he had made it there, he had thrown it all away.

Yet he could not have done otherwise, and he knew this too. He had acted as he should, as was proper. And so he felt serene as he stared into the Commissario's limpid green eyes, blinking in the strong morning light that came through the window. He thought that the investigator, despite the abominable work he did and the situation in which he found himself, was an honest man, worthy of respect. In the first place, he looked directly at you, looked you in the eye, and it was uncommon to meet people who did that. Then too, he felt that he had suffered, like him. And finally, he had called him back. Instead of being satisfied with the confession, he wanted to get to the bottom of it, to understand. And that meant that he was intelligent. An intelligent, honest cop: a rare and dangerous thing.

Ricciardi looked at Nespoli in silence. With a nod he had dismissed the policeman who had brought him in and had remained seated, hands clasped in front of his mouth, elbows leaning on the desk. Nespoli held his gaze, standing with his hands cuffed in front of him. After a long moment, Ricciardi spoke.

"Nespoli, I know everything. I figured it out. I realized it last night. I don't know if you're aware of what you're doing, what's in store for you. You'll go to jail for thirty years, you'll be an old man when you get out, that's if you get out. A man like you isn't capable of spending thirty years in the company of criminals."

Nespoli stared at him. Not so much as a breath escaped him.

"You didn't kill him. I know it. And I also know who did kill him."

The singer blinked, but didn't say a word.

"Think about those who love you: you must have a mother, brothers and sisters. I can't believe you don't have a reason, even just one, to want to live, to be free. Even if it were only to sing. You're gifted; I heard you yesterday."

Nespoli didn't move a muscle. A tear ran from his right eye and began trickling down his cheek. He seemed not to be aware of it.

"Is your relationship with this woman that compelling? What has she done for you, to deserve this sacrifice? Why are you giving her your life?"

The man in handcuffs went on staring boldly into Ricciardi's eyes; in the heat of the argument the Commissario leaned forwards.

"If you don't help me, how can I help you? I can't continue working on the case if you don't retract your confession. Let me at least try. Don't let me be the one to send an innocent man to prison. Please. Retract it."

Nespoli gave a faint, sad smile and said nothing. After another long moment, Ricciardi sighed deeply.

"As you wish. I thought you would react this way." He called the guard and said: "Take him away."

On the way out, Nespoli paused in the doorway, turned and said softly: "Thank you, Commissario. If you've ever been in love, you understand me."

I understand you, Ricciardi thought.

After a few minutes, Ponte knocked at the door.

"Excuse me, Commissario. The Vice Questore would like to speak with you in his office."

Sighing wearily, Ricciardi got up and walked to the spacious office at the end of the hall. Even before he reached the partly open door he perceived the wild pungent scent of spices; by now he recognized it. Garzo had someone with him.

"Ah, my dear Ricciardi! Please, come in. Have a seat. You've already met Signora Vezzi, haven't you?"

Sitting in front of the Vice Questore was Livia, legs crossed, dressed as usual in a sober yet sensual dark suit. The little veil on her hat was raised; she was smoking. Her splendid dark eyes gazed steadily at Ricciardi and her mouth bore the hint of a smile. She looked like a panther, ready to fall asleep or attack her prey, not caring which.

"Signora Vezzi saw the good news about the killer's arrest in the newspaper," Garzo said, "and came to offer her congratulations. She said she will express her satisfaction in the circles of Rome's highest authorities, to which she has access. Even to our beloved *Duce* himself, since she is a friend of his and of his wife. She wanted to see you, to congratulate you."

Ricciardi remained standing and looked straight at Livia. Continuing to stare at her, he addressed his words to Garzo.

"Signora Vezzi attributes excessive importance to the work we've done. We should have continued to investigate further, actually. Perhaps we were simply . . . fortunate, to come upon a confession."

Garzo assumed a worried tone, giving Ricciardi a dirty look; it was lost on him, however, since the Commissario was still looking at the widow.

"What are you talking about? As usual, our Ricciardi is too modest. Actually, our arrest was the result of a very thorough and, as the newspaper says, tireless investigation. I myself—and the signora will be so kind as to keep it in mind so as to be able to report it—gave frequent procedural instructions to the Commissario and, on the basis of these instructions, we were able to catch the perpetrator; who confessed only when he found himself backed into a corner by the irrefutable evidence that we gathered. Isn't that right, Ricciardi?"

Garzo's tone was now definitely menacing. Livia went on smiling, smoking and watching Ricciardi.

"I have no doubt that your . . . teamwork, as they say, produced the result. But I myself have had the opportunity to observe Commissario Ricciardi first-hand and I can testify that nothing distracts him from his work. He is a topnotch man."

Garzo was not willing to be shunted aside and tried to ride the wave as usual.

"Indeed, he is one of our best men. This success, a collaborative effort based on teamwork, as you noted, Signora, is due primarily to the ability to choose the right people to appoint to the right places. Isn't that so, Ricciardi?"

The Commissario had not taken his eyes off Livia, who in turn had not stopped looking at him and smiling. Called upon once again, he couldn't help but respond.

"Vice Questore Garzo is correct. Whatever he has said, may say or will say. As for me, the signora knows that I do what I must do. At least I try to. May I go now?"

Livia nodded, still smiling.

Garzo growled: "Yes, Ricciardi, go. And remember what we talked about before."

Ricciardi briefly bowed his head by way of goodbye and left.

# XXXI

A couple of hours later, Maione's son, a boy of sixteen whom the Commissario had seen with his father several times, knocked on Ricciardi's door.

"Good morning, Commissario. Papa asks if you can join him at Caffè Gambrinus in Piazza Plebiscito. He says he has to talk to you."

"Thank you. I'm on my way."

Maione looked even more like a policeman in plain clothes than when he was in uniform. Ricciardi couldn't have said why. Maybe it was the way he wore his hat, or his rigid bearing. The fact was you couldn't go wrong: he was a cop. He was waiting for him at the usual table, the one where Ricciardi sat to eat his *sfogliatella* at lunchtime. When the Commissario arrived, he started to get up, but Ricciardi stopped him with a gesture and sat down as well.

"I ordered coffee and a *sfogliatella* for you."

"Thanks. Look, it's on me; you haven't received that bonus yet. He's grown, your son. My compliments. He resembles his . . . his mother."

"He resembles his brother, Luca, *Commissa'*. You can say it; you think I don't see it with my own eyes? He looks just like him. The other day he told me he too wants to be a policeman. His mother fled to the bedroom, crying. I had to slap him hard. I yelled at him: 'Don't ever say that again!' This is a rotten job. A criminal is better off."

"Don't be silly: don't say such things. The boy should do

what he wants. Obviously, with this pig-headed father of his as an example, it's only natural that he would want to be a policeman."

"And maybe even a commissario—no offence."

"None taken. So then, what have you come up with?"

"I saw Bambinella, I even went to where he lives, in San Nicola da Tolentino. You should have seen him: he was wearing a woman's dressing gown, his hair swept up with a barrette. Since I'm used to seeing him in make-up, I didn't even recognize him. '*Brigadie'*, such a pleasure! So, you've made up your mind at last?' One more word and I would have punched him! He says that to me of all people! Anyway, he let me into the basement apartment where he lives and even offered me a surrogate. I explained what we needed and he already knew all about it. It seems that our friend is quite famous in the Quartieri. Actually, Bambinella immediately asked me why I needed the information. I told him that, to begin with, I needed it so I wouldn't have to send him to prison for indecent assault and he said: 'Okay, I get it, at your service, *Brigadie'*.' And he talked."

Ricciardi smiled briefly, taking a bite of *sfogliatella*.

"And why is the signorina quite famous?"

"Because she's beautiful, first of all. Then too, because she can read and write. She teaches the kids who don't go to school, which is most of them. Also, and here it gets interesting, because for several months she was living with a man—Bambinella doesn't know his real name—whom they called *'o Cantante*, the Singer. In fact, she's even known as *'a 'nnammurata d'o Cantante*, the Singer's sweetheart, even though they no longer live together."

"And how long ago did they stop living together?"

Maione consulted his notes on a slip of paper he had pulled out of his coat pocket.

"More or less since Christmas, he says."

"More or less since Christmas, of course. It's natural."

"Why, natural?"

"Because it all started at Christmas. Things with Vezzi started at Christmas. And the signorina threw *'o Cantante* out of the house, using some excuse. And guess who *'o Cantante* is?"

"*Commissa'*, *'o Cantante* is Nespoli. Who else, if not him?"

Ricciardi used his fingers to wipe the sugar off his lips and nodded.

"Right, Nespoli. And there's our reconstruction of his mysterious past, where he lived before moving to his current apartment. Go on."

"She lives alone now. She leads a somewhat withdrawn life, she doesn't get too familiar with anyone. However, there's news and it's big news: the signorina is expecting, *Commissa'*. She's pregnant. She confided it to the caretaker, because a few nights ago she was sick, she threw up, the usual thing. Would you believe it, *Commissa'*? When Bambinella told me, he was green with envy!"

Ricciardi had leaned forward as he always did when his full attention was captured.

"Pregnant, huh? There it is: the tame animal who becomes a beast. And did you ask about the other thing I told you to ask about?"

"Of course, *Commissa'*: you were right, as usual." Maione smiled admiringly, shaking his head. "The young lady writes with her left hand."

The afternoon passed slowly, as the wind continued to rattle the city.

Ricciardi remained shut up in his office, trying to take care of some routine paperwork he had neglected over the past few days, but he found it hard to concentrate. In his mind, the chain of events was now complete. But the Incident did not entirely fit the picture that had been formed. Vezzi was singing Nespoli's aria: why so, if the baritone, as Ricciardi believed, had not committed the murder? And why was Vezzi crying? It was uncommon in Ricciardi's experience: a sudden, violent death left no time for emotion. The tears must have preceded it. So then, why was Vezzi crying when he was killed? The Commissario glanced frequently at the clock. He had an appointment with someone who didn't know she had an appointment with him, and he couldn't be late.

The wind was still blowing fiercely, howling beneath the portico of the San Carlo. Standing around the corner, with his collar up and his hair tossed about, Ricciardi imagined how that place would be without the insistent whistling. Each time he had been there, in the past three days, the wind had virtually never let up. In the distance you could even hear the roar of the sea, when a rare car or a rattling tram wasn't going by.

He hadn't been waiting long when the person he was waiting for came out of the door to the gardens, along with two other women Ricciardi recognized: Maria and Addolorata. He looked at the petite figure of the young woman he wanted to talk to. What a miscalculation he had made, the first time he had seen her. Insignificant, struggling under the weight of the hanger that held the clown's costume. Eyes downcast, shoulders curved. The woman who had stopped Vezzi's heart and stolen that of Nespoli; whose single long blonde hair was on the dressing gown in the boarding house in the Vomero; who had lived with the penniless baritone then threw him out of the house at Christmas, when she had begun a relationship with the wealthy tenor: Maddalena Esposito at your service, *Commissa'*.

The woman saw him and stopped. Perhaps, for a moment, she even thought of running. Then she hastily said goodbye to her co-workers and came towards him. When she stood before him, she looked directly at him. The woman's eyes were blue, intense and clear. She was very pretty, Ricciardi only then realized. How could he have noticed it before, he thought, since she didn't usually show it. Only when and if it suited her.

"Good evening, *Commissa'*. What a surprise, to find you here."

"Good evening to you, Signorina. Shall we take a walk?"

The woman seemed curious.

"Are you here in an official capacity, or not?"

"It depends. It depends on you. I'd say no."

Maddalena nodded, then turned towards the piazza and began walking.

They went a few hundred yards in silence. Ricciardi knew that it would be up to him to lay his cards on the table first, otherwise the woman would hide behind Nespoli's confession. Nor did he have any intention of underestimating Maddalena's intelligence; she had successfully managed to conceal her role in the affair from the beginning.

"May I offer you some coffee? This wind makes it difficult to talk."

Maddalena glanced quickly at him and nodded. A dark kerchief covered her hair and a coarse scarf was wound around her neck and mouth; she wore a dark threadbare coat, turned inside out with her skilled seamstress' hands. They found an open café inside Galleria Umberto and sat down at a table away from the others.

The woman took off her coat and kerchief and folded them neatly on her lap. Ricciardi looked at her for some time. Her hands were slim and delicate, like her facial features; her hair, pulled up and bound, had a natural golden colour, like her eyebrows, and her complexion was dark, an unusual and pleasing contrast. What was surprising, however, were her eyes: a deep blue, with yellow flecks, they reminded him of those of a cat. Seeing them, the Commissario understood why the woman always keep them lowered and carefully avoided aiming them directly at anyone who looked at her: she could never have gone unnoticed.

"I could pretend and tell you that Nespoli gave us your

name. Or I could interrogate you and make you confess. I don't think you can afford a lawyer good enough to defend you against the charges of the court. But I looked into your man's eyes and I want to respect his wishes. I know what happened, it's clear to me; I cannot allow that young man to go to prison for thirty years as a result of this lie, for something he didn't do, or that he didn't do alone. So, I want to understand. Explain it to me."

He fixed his cool green eyes on the girl's blue, limpid ones: two minds, two intellects confronting one another. Without pretence, without masks.

The woman placed a hand on her stomach, gently.

"You know . . . "

A statement, not a question. He nodded.

"My name is Esposito because I was abandoned when I was born. Did you know that almost all abandoned children die? Only the strong ones survive, *Commissa'*. Those who are very strong. I've been through illness, hunger. I was given up for dead maybe ten times, not that anyone would have cared much. Instead I survived: by tooth and nail. It surprised everyone, this little shrimp of a girl clinging so firmly to life. Then, because I wanted to survive, I learned to read and write. I would go and sit beside the nun who did the accounts; she didn't even speak to me, but I watched her. Sewing, too. I watched the nun who kept mending the same little smocks over and over again; later on I helped her, while the other girls played or died from disease. And the hunger: I don't even want to tell you what I ate when I was little, to survive. The most horrible things."

Ricciardi looked at her and thought, there it was, the same old enemy: hunger.

"But the others were dying, even that the ones who seemed strong. Smallpox, cholera. Typhoid, diphtheria. How many diseases do you want, *Commissa'*? I can tell you all about them, even better than a doctor. And then one morning I felt ready and I left. Without thanking anyone, without taking anything away with me. What could I have taken? I had nothing. And what should I have thanked them for? They had given me nothing. I slept in the streets, I ate with the dogs, I defended myself. They didn't want me even at the brothel: I was too skinny, I wore the face of hunger. Still, there was something I knew how to do: I could cut and sew. With my left hand."

She raised her left hand in front of his face, looking at it as if it were a trophy, a medal. Ricciardi felt a remote quiver in his heart, thinking of a small hand that embroidered.

"I worked for a tailor, an old goat who took advantage of me. I let him do it, I had to eat. I waited for it to end. I slept in the doorway of the shop. Then one day Signora Lilla came in. She wanted a length of fabric in a colour that she had seen in the window. All it took her was a moment, one look. She has great foresight, Signora Lilla does. She saw that I was skilful, that I worked hard, and that the man was a pig. She called me aside. The next day I was working at the San Carlo."

She said it as though she had gone to heaven. In spite of himself, Ricciardi could picture the young woman's life and he felt sorry for her. But in his mind Vezzi's image sang and wept over the years that he had yet to live, that he would not live.

"There was light, warmth, even music. I had never heard music before, *Commissa'*. A few piano chords, the radio from balcony windows left open in the summer. But that kind of music, never. It captures your soul, it makes you feel alive. And then they laughed, they danced. And they paid me besides! To be in such festive surroundings! Me, who until just the day before had been fighting rats and dogs over the scraps! I never wanted to leave. I worked late, I was the first to arrive in the morning. Signora Lilla spoke with a friend of hers who drives a carriage: he had a vacant room above the Quartieri, converted from an attic. A place to live! I felt like a countess."

The woman's eyes were dreamy, as if she were recounting a fairy tale. The steaming cup of coffee sat in front of her; she hadn't even taken a sip of it.

"My life went on that way for two years. I became very proficient, *Commissa'*: the best. But I didn't want to ruin everything by standing out, things were fine the way they were. I help the other girls when they're unable to do something; I take the more complicated work for myself. That way everyone likes me. I make sure no one notices me, because I know, I learned it well throughout my life, that if they notice you, sooner or later they'll do something bad to you. And I was right."

A shadow passed over the rapt, stunning blue eyes, like a sudden dark cloud in the sky. Maddalena sighed and continued.

"I found Michele one evening when I came back from work, very late: *La Traviata* was the next day, the costumes for the party scene are difficult. He was on the ground, inside the door, I nearly stepped on him. He looked dead. What could I do? I had been dying too, of hunger, lying in so many doorways. Could I say the hell with him, let him die just to avoid any trouble? No. How would I have been able to sleep anymore? So I helped him. I brought him upstairs. In other neighbourhoods, in other buildings, they wouldn't have let me do that. But here, in this city, no offence, *Commissa'*, those who are hard up are often better than the cops. Needy people, those who are on the run, or hungry, help each other. We survive that way, closely bound to one another. Because we know, *Commissa'*, that if we don't help each other, nobody else will help us. And so, if Michele is alive, he's alive because of me. And because of the neighbours in the building, and those on our street. Because of the district. And he knows it, he's well aware of it. That was what you saw in his eyes."

Ricciardi was all too familiar with the balance of powers in the city. He was painfully aware of what the woman was saying and of the impossibility of changing the way things were.

"It was all so natural. Michele is handsome, kind and good. He too has suffered a lot and he's still suffering. He recovered, he stayed with me. I care for him, he cares for me, and it's the first time for both of us. I spoke with Signora Lilla, who spoke with Lasio, the stage manager, who in turn spoke with the orchestra director, Maestro Pelosi. No one there knew about us two; I told them that a friend of mine had heard him sing in a trattoria. They hired him right away, as soon as they heard him: the voice of an angel."

Ricciardi could hear the pride in Maddalena's voice. He was trying to figure out how the woman felt about Nespoli. She was attached to him, of course, but she wasn't quivering with passion.

"They wouldn't have hired him if they'd known he was living with someone he wasn't married to. In these circles that's how it is, *Commissa'*. So he found a place of his own."

"And as luck would have it, he found it just when you met Vezzi for the first time."

The woman flinched; she lowered her eyes a moment, then looked up and gave the Commissario a defiant glare.

"That's right: when I met Arnaldo Vezzi. The father of my child."

# XXXII

As if to dramatically underscore the woman's words, a gust of wind blew through the Galleria, shaking the window of the café.

"And you're sure of that?"

Maddalena smiled sadly.

"With someone like me, you have to ask that, right? With a woman like me, the child can be anybody's. The first guy who comes along. But not your girlfriend, right? You wouldn't ask your girlfriend a question like that."

Now it was Ricciardi who smiled sadly.

"No, I wouldn't. Not that or any other question. Excuse me. Go on."

"That day, Signora Lilla had a backache. Actually it wasn't true, she just didn't want to deal with Vezzi. No one wanted to have anything to do with him. When he'd come to Naples, two years earlier I think, he had got two people fired; he said they were incompetent. That's how he was. Only he existed. Measurements had to be taken for the *Pagliacci* costumes; they had to be ready for the current performance. We always work like that, two or three months in advance. At Christmas, Vezzi arrived, then in January, the other members of the company came. Anyway, he was extremely particular; he wanted to see everything, the staging, the props, every single thing. Especially his costumes.

"I was talking with Michele when he arrived. Outside the entrance to the theater. I remember it as though it were today.

I hadn't seen him before. He stepped out of the car with two others: he was tall, big, and wore a hat and scarf. He wasn't handsome, but he was rich. You could tell, *Commissa'*: someone who was loaded, not with money, not only that, but with power. A man who could do anything he wanted. Anything at all. At any time. He looked at us as he went in. At me and Michele. At me. And he smiled, the smile of a ferocious animal. I know that smile, *Commissa'*: men give me that smile just before they lay their hands on me. When they realize that a woman no longer has any place she can run to."

"And Nespoli, didn't he look at you that way?"

"No. Not Michele. Michele treats me as if I were a princess. For him I am a princess. I've always been one. And it was Michele who told me that he was Vezzi. His voice was shaking with excitement. He said to me: "Do you know who that is? That's Vezzi, the god among tenors." That's just what he said. The god among tenors. And he acted like he was god, *Commissa'*. If he wanted something, he took it; then, when he didn't want it anymore, he threw it away. And if he couldn't take something away from someone else, it was of no interest to him."

"And you, he had seen you with Nespoli."

"Yes, he had seen me with Michele. And he told me later that he had seen how we looked at each other, specifically how Michele looked at me. He said, 'The young man's eyes were burning: he looked like he wanted to eat you.' And he, being god, couldn't stand to have a man look at a woman like that in his presence, because he had to be the only one. That's what stray dogs are like, I've dealt with them in the streets. That's how he was. Worse than a dog. Dogs don't laugh."

"And then what happened?"

"What happened was that Signora Lilla sent me to Vezzi's dressing room, to do the fitting. 'You go, Maddalena,' she said. 'The way I'm feeling today, I'll get myself thrown out of the theater, with that ill-mannered lunatic.' Instead, with me he was very kind. He didn't take any liberties, or lay a hand on me. He talked, he talked a lot. He told me that he was lonely and sad. That he no longer even spoke to his wife, hadn't for years. That with all the people he had around him, there wasn't a single person who really cared for him. That if he ever had the good fortune of being with a real woman again, he would never let her go. That he wanted a son."

Unexpectedly, Maddalena laughed. A bleak laugh, one that held tears. Ricciardi looked out of the window.

"He wanted a son. He had lost his, he said, because his wife hadn't taken care of him, she hadn't noticed his high fever in time. He was good, *Commissa'*. He was so good at acting. Maybe, after years of singing onstage, he thought that life was all an act. All a game. And I, clever Maddalena, the one who had survived hunger, thirst and disease, who had battled dogs, rats and men, fell for it. The next day, I sent word that I wasn't feeling well, I told Michele that I was going to visit an elderly nun who was sick, and I spent the day in the Vomero, with him. And the next day as well. We forgot about the world, in that room in the Vomero."

"The Pensione Belvedere."

Maddalena gave him a tired smile.

"You know about that, too. Did you go inside the room, did you see it? Then you've also seen the place where I was happy, the only place in my life where I was truly happy. He called me his blonde fairy, he caressed my eyes and stroked my hair. He told me that my suffering was over, that he would leave his wife and the entire world to be with me. That he would give it to me on a silver platter, the world."

"And you believed him."

"And I believed him. Because I wanted to believe. Because such things can happen, even in life. A friend of mine married a hardware dealer; she used to live above a brothel at the

Sanità and now she acts like a great lady and if she sees me on the street she pretends she doesn't know me. Couldn't that happen to me as well?"

"And what about Nespoli, didn't you think of him?"

Maddalena's expression was stricken, as if she'd felt a sharp pain.

"Michele . . . we were two poor devils, Michele and me. What future could we have had? Even if he were successful, where could he go with someone like me with him? What future was there for us? Anyway, I wasn't his. I had become Arnaldo's, from the very moment he'd looked at me. When he left, he told me that he would put his affairs in order and come back for me. That I must not say a word to anyone, meanwhile, because otherwise his wife, who knew important people, would take steps to prevent us from being together. That I must be careful and wait patiently. And I waited patiently. I believed him. I thought he was a harsh man because he was lonely, and that with me he would become the sweetest man in the world. And I watched him leave and I went back to my everyday life. Which was no longer enough for me, however."

"Nespoli included."

"Including Michele, yes. It all seemed so . . . paltry, so empty. Even things that before had seemed heavenly. I was dreaming of jewels, furs. But more than anything, I dreamed about Arnaldo, a prince who made me feel like a queen. And Michele . . . Michele wanted to marry me. I didn't feel I could say no, tell him it wasn't possible; he frightened me. Michele is dangerous: he has a peculiar temperament, he can become violent. I told him it was better to wait until he became a success."

"And then you discovered . . . "

"Yes, a month later. I was so happy, *Commissa'*! I thought I would be giving Arnaldo the son he had lost, that I would be offering him a family and contentment. I didn't try to contact him, I didn't write to him. I knew he would be coming, that the performance was scheduled for this time, and I waited. I waited so I could tell him myself; I wanted to see the expression on his face. I wouldn't have missed it for anything in the world."

"Did you approach him right away, when he came?"

"Yes, of course. I went up to him as soon as he got to the theater, the second day he was here, to prepare for the dress rehearsal. He told me we had to be careful, that his secretary spied on him and reported back to his wife, that we would see each other the following day, the day of the rehearsal, at the Pensione Belvedere. I told him which tram he should take, if he came in a carriage or by taxi everyone would notice. And we saw each other there."

"Did you tell him then?"

"No. He was tired, edgy. I didn't want to tell him when he was that way. It was such a beautiful thing, so important that I didn't want to throw it away. He fell asleep and when he woke up it was so late that he nearly missed the dress rehearsal. I said goodbye and told him I loved him. Then we went to the theater, separately."

Ricciardi leaned forward, aware that they had reached the critical point.

"And so, we come to the night of the twenty-fifth."

Maddalena visibly shuddered and glanced around. Then she looked steadily at Ricciardi, placing a hand on her stomach again.

"I have to know what you intend to do, Commissario. I don't have only myself to think about. I won't let my child be born in prison: you know what happens. They give the baby to an institution and if he survives, he survives the way I survived. I won't let my child have the kind of life I had. Well then?"

Ricciardi knew that Maddalena was right and he also knew that her child was innocent. He thought about Nespoli, however, and the tear that had run down his cheek that morning. And about Vezzi's tears. Did he have the right to grant pardon on their behalf?

"I don't want to see a baby born in prison either. That much I can tell you. But I don't want to see an innocent man sent to prison for thirty years, whose only crime was to love a woman. One who used him."

Maddalena flushed.

"I was only trying to protect my child. I wanted— I want to give him a better life."

Ricciardi had not taken his eyes off those of the woman for one second.

"Go on."

There was a momentary silence. The woman knew the Commissario would not let up until he had learned the truth. All she could do was tell him how it had happened and place her hope in the glimmer of humanity she perceived in those gleaming green eyes. She thought back to three days before; she relived her grief for the hundredth time.

"I went straight to his dressing room. He had already put on his make-up. How strange he was with his clown's face. Not that I didn't like him. I still liked him. He smiled at me, nervously. He seemed distant. I thought it was because of the performance. A great singer is great because he's always tense before measuring up to his own talent again. I looked at him, smiled at him. And I told him. Just like that, simply: we were going to have a child. He looked at me, with the powder puff in his hand. He looked as though he hadn't understood. Then he frowned and asked me why I hadn't been careful. I didn't understand: wasn't it the most beautiful thing in the world? Wasn't he happy too, the way I was happy? He said there was nothing to worry about, he would give me the money. I didn't get it, what was he talking about? Killing our baby? Hadn't he already lost a child?

"He clawed my arm, he hurt me. He shouted that I mustn't dare talk about his son. I reminded him of his promises, it was he who had told me that we would be together, forever.

"He let go of my arm then, stepped back and began to laugh. Softly, at first. A little chuckle, like when you think of something funny. Then louder and louder: unrestrained, vulgar peals of laughter. He was gasping, saying 'You and I, together . . . someone like me, with someone like you . . . may I introduce my new wife, Madame Needle-and-Thread . . . my son, the son of a seamstress . . . ' and he laughed and laughed. He was doubled over . . . "

*. . . doubled over, on his knees . . .*

" . . . He looked like he had lost his senses. He had his hand stretched out, as if he wanted to hold me off because I was making him laugh . . . "

*. . . hand outstretched, as if to ward off . . .*

" . . . And all the while, he laughed and laughed. He laughed so hard that tears came to his eyes. He was crying, that's how hard he was laughing . . . !"

*. . . tears, rolling down his face . . .*

" . . . He wouldn't stop! And I felt my feelings for him change. I felt his deceitfulness. Outside, from the stage, I heard Michele singing. I heard Michele's love and the laughter of the Pagliaccio in front of me. I could feel my hatred coursing through my veins, infecting me."

*. . . Io sangue voglio, all'ira m'abbandono, in odio tutto l'amor mio finì* . . . I will have vengeance . . . and all my love shall end in hate . . .

" . . . And then my hand seized the scissors I had around my neck, my seamstress' shears, and I stabbed him hard, a single blow, to the throat. I don't know if I meant to kill him. Maybe I just wanted him to stop laughing."

*. . . A blow with the scissors. That's what was missing when I saw you. And with your left hand, because you're left-handed like my Enrica. Therefore on the right side of the clown's neck as he stood in front of you. In the carotid . . .*

"He stopped laughing, in fact. He was gurgling with his

hand at his throat, that oh-so-precious throat. I sat on the sofa, under the gushing blood. I wanted to see how a Pagliaccio dies."

. . . *The clean cushion, the only one. You were sitting on it. Watching the clown die. I will have vengeance . . .*

" . . . Then, as though in a dream, I opened the door to leave. At that moment, Michele came down from the stage. I don't know if God exists, Commissario. But it's truly strange that just at that moment, with all the coming and going there is from the dressing rooms during the performance, Michele, my Michele, should be the only one who saw me. And he saw me wide-eyed, my smock drenched with Vezzi's blood, the scissors in my fist, torn from their ribbon. He pushed me back into the dressing room.

"He looked around, he understood. By this time Vezzi had no more blood, but he was still wheezing, a death rattle. So Michele punched him in the face . . . "

. . . *Haematoma too small for a fracture, the doctor had said; the victim had no more blood . . .*

" . . . and he told me to take off my bloodstained smock. Then he wrapped the scissors in the smock, broke the mirror and propped Vezzi on the chair. He took the sharpest fragment and stuck it into the wound on his neck, all the way in, holding it with the stained smock. I watched as though I were looking out of the window. Then he told me to wait there, and locked the door. He took Vezzi's coat, scarf and hat from the armoire and put them on. He grabbed the smock and scissors and shoved them under his coat. And he jumped down from the window . . . "

. . . *To get rid of any trace of you at the crime scene. So that no one would think it might have been you . . .*

" . . . I waited with the body. I felt like I was in a dream. After a minute, or maybe a year, I heard Michele's whisper outside the door. I opened it, to let him in . . . "

*. . . After he had bumped into don Pierino on the stairs, who mistook him for Vezzi . . .*

" . . . He told me he had to switch his shoes, which were muddied: otherwise he would leave tracks on the stage, where he would shortly return. That's when I woke up: I realized I had to hurry, that I could save my child from ruin. This time, he waited for me in the dressing room and I went up to the fourth floor. I said I had come straight from the sick nun's convent and I asked Maria to lend me her smock . . . "

*. . . Too big for you, as I recall . . .*

" . . . I got the shoes and brought them down. No one notices us seamstresses when we come and go. I held them under the smock, which was too big for me. Michele put the clean ones on and gave me the muddy ones and I went upstairs again to put them back in place. He took care of the keys . . . "

*. . . The locked door, that Lasio had to break down . . .*

" . . . Then I took the costume and told Signora Lilla that it was ready. I had finished it. I had made the final adjustment, the final cut."

*. . . The final cut.*

# XXXIII

The wind was whipping through the Galleria, relentlessly. Now that Maddalena was silent, it sounded even stronger. Time seemed to stand still. The woman stared into space and saw her own ghosts; the only thing keeping her moored to the present was her hand resting on her stomach.

Ricciardi shifted in his chair and drew her attention.

"Signorina, listen to me carefully. Your destiny, that of Nespoli and above all that of your child are forever bound. You cannot think of building the child's life around a lie and on the punishment of an innocent man."

Maddalena went on staring into space.

"I know a lawyer who owes me a favour. He'll see to defending Nespoli, who, if he sticks to his current story, hasn't a chance. If he were to change it, however, there could still be some hope."

The woman roused herself and looked at the Commissario.

"Hope? For Michele? What hope?"

"Honour killings are punishable by imprisonment up to a maximum of three years. You will have to say—and this is my condition for letting you go free—that Nespoli intervened because Vezzi tried to sexually assault you and you called for help."

"And me? My child?"

"Nothing at all will happen to you. You're a victim. The concealment of evidence will fall on Nespoli and impact his sentence. You must say that you two were about to be married.

That you told Vezzi that when he made his first advances, which you firmly rejected. That you didn't tell us everything right away because you were afraid, because you're pregnant, and the child is Michele's."

Maddalena started.

"But it's not true, I know it!"

"Believe me, the child can only benefit from it. In any case, you have no choice. The alternative is prison."

The woman lowered her head, considering the gravity of the situation. She had no other options.

"I understand, *Commissa'*. It's only fair, it has to be this way. I'll wait for Michele. But will the judges believe these things? Vezzi was an important figure and we're just modest people. What hope do we have?"

She looked at Ricciardi, and all of a sudden big tears began to flow from those limpid blue eyes.

As he skirted the Royal Palace, struggling against the stiff wind that hampered his progress, Ricciardi was thinking about hunger and love. This time the two old enemies had joined forces to perpetrate their crime. He had left Maddalena, vulnerable and alone, with her kerchief covering her blonde hair and the assurance that tomorrow, after work, she would appear at the lawyer's office. Ricciardi himself would inform him of events. And it wouldn't cost her anything. Then he decided that the long day wasn't yet over.

The sky was clear, swept by the wind. The moon and stars lit up the deserted street, while the lights hanging in the centre of the road swayed wildly. Love. A sometimes fatal illness, but a necessary one. Maybe you can't live without it, Ricciardi thought as he walked against the wind, his hands in his coat pockets. Eyes peered at him from dark alleys, recognized him and decided that he was not an opportune prey for the final pickpocket of the day. Now he was at the corner of Via

Partenope. To his left the sea's high waves crashed on the reef. On the right were the big hotels.

At home, in her kitchen, Enrica had finished doing the dishes with her usual meticulous attention. She had already checked the window across the way a number of times: its curtains were closed. Tonight she felt an anxiety that wrung her heart, though she didn't know why. She felt alone, abandoned. Where are you tonight, my love?

Livia watched the sea's fury from her window on the third floor of the Hotel Excelsior. She was smoking and thinking. Tomorrow she would leave the city and try to resume her life once again. Would she find the strength? She glanced at her suitcase, already packed and ready to go. What am I taking away from here? And what am I leaving in this city, with its sea howling in the wind?

Her thoughts did not go to Arnaldo; she felt as though she had never known him. What she saw through the smoke was a pair of feverish green eyes. The arrogance, the disillusionment in those eyes. The loneliness and yearning for love deep in that soul. And the sorrow: that immense sorrow. Why didn't you let me relieve that sorrow? Inhaling a last mouthful of smoke, she looked again at the riotous sea. In the surge of foam that sprayed on to the street, she saw a figure walking against the wind. She recognized it. And her heart leaped into her throat.

The clerk at the hotel reception desk did not want to notify Signora Vezzi. That wet, dishevelled man, his green eyes raging with fever, frightened him. He was thinking of calling a couple of porters to help chase him out, when the signora stepped out of the elevator, breathless. Livia's eyes were lit up, shining. She had thrown her coat on over her dressing gown, run a comb through her soft, thick dark hair, slipped on some shoes and rushed down. Her heart was pounding in her ears, her mouth was dry. He had come to her.

Enrica sat down in her chair and took out her embroidery box. Another glance at the window. Nothing. Her anxiety would not let up. She felt like crying.

Ricciardi looked at Livia: she had never seemed so beautiful. The luminous eyes, the full lips smiling broadly. He told her that he had to speak with her. It was important. She asked him where he wanted to talk, and he said, "Let's walk."

Outside, they found themselves accompanied by the wind and sea. The lights hanging in the centre of the road swayed, illuminating at times one side or the other. Livia shivered and clutched Ricciardi's arm. He began to speak.

"The truth is not what it seems, sometimes. In fact, it hardly ever is. It's a bit like the strange light of these lamps, you see, Livia: sometimes it falls here, sometimes there. Never on both sides at the same time. So you have to imagine what you don't see. You have to intuit it from a word, spoken or unspoken, from a trace, an impression. From a note, sometimes.

"Those who do my kind of work have another eye: they're able to see things that others can't see. And that's how it was this time, Livia. It didn't seem right that someone like your husband should have died because of an insult, a remark. And in fact, he did not die for that reason. Do you want to know why your husband died? He died because of hunger and because of love. That's why he died. I'll tell you about it."

Livia listened to Ricciardi's voice, mingled with those of the wind and sea. She no longer felt cold. She was walking down dark streets, eating scraps in doorways, surrounded by rats and stray dogs. She was learning to sew beside an elderly nun. She wanted to sing, in a village in the mountains, in Calabria. She slapped an elderly professor at the Conservatory. She felt the hands of a horrible old goat of a tailor on her. She fell under the spell, once again, of a rich and famous tenor. Once again she carried his child in her womb, a child who was still alive, and not yet born. And again, all that blood.

Ricciardi's voice lulled Livia; she wasn't even aware of the tears streaming down her face along with the sea spray carried by the wind. She walked along, clutching the strong arm of the sorrowful man with the upturned coat collar, sensing all his love for the suffering of others.

"Do you see, Livia? If there isn't someone in court to say who Arnaldo Vezzi really was, they'll slam this young man in Poggioreale and never let him out again. And the girl will remain alone, because in this city no one will want a penniless, dishonoured woman. And the child will be fodder for the criminal world, in the best of cases, if he doesn't die first, under the wheels of a carriage or killed by some disease."

Livia took a few more steps, then said to the wind and the upturned coat collar: "And I, what can I do? Don't you see that I am now the honoured widow of a great man? I would become a vile ingrate who spits on someone who can no longer defend himself."

"Think of the child, Livia. Think of the opportunity you have to give this child a family and a hope for the future. If you want, if you like, think about your child as well, about what he would ask you to do, if he were alive."

The woman squeezed the arm she was clinging to. She sighed in the wind that blew her hair about.

"And you? What about you? Don't you have a hope for the future? Why not give me your hope, let it become mine as well?"

They walked on in silence. They found themselves back at the entrance to the hotel. The desk clerk, behind the glass door, looked at them, puzzled.

Ricciardi stopped and looked at Livia, there in the wind and sea.

"It's not my time, Livia. Not my place. You have a right to be happy, you're entitled to the good fortune that you haven't had. You're beautiful, Livia, and young. You have that right; I don't yet."

Livia looked at him through the drops of sea spray and tears, and smiled.

"All right. I'll be there too, in court. I'll do it for my Carletto. And for you."

And she stood and watched him walk away, in the wind and sea.

The young woman who sat embroidering felt the grip of anxiety loosen in her chest. Even before raising her eyes from the embroidered pattern, she knew that the curtains in the window across the way had opened.

As she went on embroidering, Enrica smiled.

## Translator's Afterword

The year is 1931, the period of Mussolini's fascist regime. In fact, the regulation portraits hanging in Commissario Ricciardi's office (Chapter III) are those of the King and *Il Duce*: the wry references are to the small physical stature of Victor Emmanuel III of the House of Savoy, King of Italy from 1900 to 1946, and to Mussolini, known as *Mascellone* or Big Jaw, and his cult of macho strength. The 'so-called coffee' at the end of that chapter was an ersatz coffee used at that time, a coffee substitute made from roasted grain.

*Pizza fritta* (Chapter IV), Ricciardi's favourite lunch when he's not enjoying a *sfogliatella*, is a popular Neapolitan street food that enjoys a cult-like reverence among the locals: the toppings are sealed between two layers of pizza dough and deep-fried until crispy.

The "little monk," *munaciello* in Neapolitan dialect (Chapter V), is the bizarre spirit who always behaves in an unpredictable way and who is the source of infinite urban legends and popular sayings.

The lines "*Io sangue voglio, all'ira m'abbandono, in odio tutto l'amor mio finì . . .* " (I will have vengeance, My rage shall know no bounds, And all my love Shall end in hate), first quoted in Chapter VI, are from *Cavalleria Rusticana*, Act One, Scene IX.

The seamstresses in the theater's wardrobe department use

charcoal irons to iron the costumes (Chapter VII): the base of these irons was a container in which glowing coals were placed to keep the iron hot.

In Chapter VIII, the Carso, Kras in Slovenian, is a plateau in southwestern Slovenia and north-eastern Italy.

The "dolesome notes" in Chapter IX are from Dante's *Inferno*, V: 25-27: "*Or incomincian le dolenti note / a farmisi sentire; or son venuto / là dove molto pianto mi percuote.*" They have been variously translated as "the dolesome notes" (Longfellow), "notes of desperation" (Mandelbaum), and even a "choir of anguish" (Ciardi).

The barefoot children racing in the wind in Chapter XII, their too-large, hand-me-down shirts billowing like sails, are playing "*barca a vela,*" pretending to be sailboats.

The crystal bottle and four cordial glasses in Garzo's office (also Chapter XII) are for serving *rosolio*, a popular Italian liqueur derived from rose petals.

The mention of Verga in Chapter XIII alludes to the fact that the libretto for *Cavalleria Rusticana* is adapted from a play written by Giovanni Verga, based on his short story of the same name; it is considered one of the classic *verismo* operas. Prevalent in late nineteenth-century Italy, veristic operas tended to feature passions which ran high and led to violence.

In the same chapter (XIII) Maione gives Ricciardi a military salute because at that time the Polizia di Stato was a military force; it became a civil force in 1981, with the enactment of Italian State Law 121.

The Funicolare Centrale (Chapter XVIII) was a funicular railway line that opened in 1928. Also in this chapter (XVIII), Irpinia, a region of the Apennine Mountains around Avellino, is mentioned as the site of the 1930 earthquake. Avellino, a town in Campania, Southern Italy, is about 25 miles east of Naples. The Pollino (chapter XXV) is a mountain range in Calabria.

The Sicilian serenade which don Pierino summarizes for the Commissario (Chapter XXVII) is in dialect: "*E si ce muoru e vaju 'n paradisu / si nun ce truovo a ttia, mancu ce trasu . . . ] [O Lola c'hai di latti la cammisa / si bianca e russa comu la cirasa, / quannu t'affacci fai la vucca a risa, / biatu pì lu primu cu ti vasa! / Ntra la puorta tua lu sangu è spasu, / ma nun me mpuorta si ce muoru accisu . . . / e si ce muoru e vaju 'n paradisu / si nun ce truovo a ttia, mancu ce trasu.*" O Lola, with your milk-white blouse, / white-skinned, with lips like cherries / your laughing face looks from the window, / and the first one to kiss you is blessed! / Blood may be spilt on your doorstep, / but to die there is nothing to me. / If, dying I went up to heaven / and found you not there I would flee!

The reference to the passing of "a rare car" (Chapter XXXI) denotes the fact that carriages or trams were the prevalent mode of transportation at the time, rather than automobiles. According to the author, Naples was a city characterized by great wealth in the hands of a few aristocrats and great poverty on the part of the proletariat; a merchant middle-class was just developing, so cars were still uncommon.

Also in Chapter XXXI, Maddalena explains that her name is Esposito because she was abandoned when she was born: the author clarified that the surname Esposito derives from the Latin 'expositus', exposed, since abandoned newborns were 'exposed', displayed, for a few hours to allow their real mothers to change their minds and reclaim them. Once that period of time was over, the orphaned babies were entrusted to the care of institutions or convents, or given up for adoption with that surname. In effect it was a kind of brand or label.

Finally, I was curious about why Ricciardi puts on a hairnet before going to bed. The author, who scrupulously researched the historic details found in the novel, explained that it was a widespread custom among the bourgeoisie of that era. Hair was washed relatively infrequently, and fixatives such as brilliantine or other preparations were commonly used. That, coupled with the fact that Ricciardi doesn't wear a hat in the blustery wind, means that he has to use a net to hold his hair in place during the night. Despite the hairnet, that wayward strand of hair insists on escaping and falling over his eyes.

Anne Milano Appel

## ACKNOWLEDGEMENTS

There are a few people Ricciardi must thank for the fact that he is here.

First of all, Francesco Pinto and Domenico Procacci, for their lucid, intrepid minds. Rosaria Carpinelli, whose attentive hand is present in the text from the first to the last word. And Aldo Putignano, a man who can fly while keeping his feet on the ground.

He must also thank Michele for his constant assistance, and Giovanni and Roberto who give meaning to everything.

Finally, speaking for myself and not just for Ricciardi, an immeasurable expression of gratitude goes to my dearest Paola.

## About the Author

Maurizio de Giovanni's Commissario Ricciardi books are bestsellers across Europe, having sold well over 1 million copies. De Giovanni is also the author of the contemporary Neapolitan thriller, *The Crocodile* (Europa, 2013), and the new contemporary Neapolitan series, *The Bastards of Pizzofalcone.* He lives in Naples with his family.

# THE COMMISSARIO RICCIARDI SERIES

The Commissario is investigating the death of one of the many street urchins who live hand-to-mouth in the dark alleys of the city. Unfortunately, his sixth sense is no help to him this time. Has his unwelcome gift finally faded? Or is something more sinister at work?

$17.00 • 9781609451875 • March 2014

In a luxurious apartment on the Mergellina beach the bodies of a Fascist militia officer and his wife have been found murdered, seemingly by two separate killers. The Commissario will have to trace a wide and frenetic arc through the streets of Naples in order to uncover the truth.

$17.00 • 9781609452063 • August 2014

Naples, 1932. At the high-class brothel in the center of town known as Paradiso, Viper, the most famous prostitute in Naples, is found smothered with a pillow. Ricciardi must untangle a complex knot of greed, frustration, jealousy, and rancor in order to solve the riddle of Viper's death.

$17.00 • 9781609452513 • March 2015

**"De Giovanni has created one of the most interesting and well-drawn detectives in fiction."—*The Daily Beast***